Annie's Quilted Mysteries™

STAB STITCHED

ELIZABETH PENNEY

Annie's®

AnniesFiction.com

Library of Congress-in-Publication Data
Stab Stitched / by Elizabeht Penney
p. cm.
I. Title
2014916582

AnniesFiction.com
(800) 282-6643
Annie's Quilted Mysteries™
Series Creator: Shari Lohner
Series Editors: Shari Lohner, Janice Tate, and Ken Tate

10 11 12 13 14 | Printed in China | 9 8 7 6 5 4 3 2

Fear tastes like a rusty knife; do not let her into your house.

—John Cheever

one

"This is a pretty nice place," Kelly Grace said, sliding over in the wooden booth so her best friend Emma Cotton could sit. Dottie Faye Sinclair, Emma's aunt, sat across from them, her huge, pink leopard-print pocketbook requiring its own spot. The threesome had met for breakfast at the Crow's Nest Café, a cozy, old-fashioned restaurant with creaking floors and beamed ceilings.

Emma glanced out the window at the thicket of sailboat masts crowding Lantern Cove's waterfront docks and moorings. Farther out in the bay, a tanker was making its stately way to Boston against a backdrop of white sails and blue water. "I like dining with a view of the ocean."

"Lantern Cove is one of the most beautiful towns on the coast," Dottie Faye said. "A lot of history here too. Wait till you see Bart's mansion." Dottie Faye had lined up a possible quilt conservation job for Emma and Kelly, who owned Cotton & Grace Quilt Designs in nearby Mystic Harbor. They designed and created original items for sale as well as restored and conserved valuable antique quilts.

"Do you think that's Olivia?" Kelly nudged Emma and nodded toward the waitress bustling toward them. In keeping with the restaurant's pirate theme, she wore a low-cut dress with puffed sleeves and full skirt suggesting a serving wench's outfit.

"I doubt it. Olivia is the owner."

They had come to Lantern Cove with dual purposes in

mind. In addition to the quilt job, they hoped to meet Olivia Stewart, one of the final suspects in their friend Rose Peterson's murder. After searching across the country, they had found her living mere miles from Mystic Harbor. By chance, Emma had seen a local newspaper article announcing Olivia's purchase of the café.

The waitress, a pretty dark-haired girl, placed three waters on the table and handed around the laminated menus she held under her arm. "Good morning, ladies. I'm Sarah, and I'll be your server. Would you like coffee?"

"Absolutely," Dottie Faye said, giving an exuberant shake of her teased blond hair. She studied the menu, one hand on the round locket she wore underneath her pink short-sleeved safari jacket. "My. These omelets look good."

"I'll take coffee too, please," Kelly said. "And I'll have the avocado and cheddar omelet, please. With home fries, sausage, and wheat toast."

Emma suppressed a smile at her friend's never-failing hearty appetite. It was a wonder that the trim brunette stayed as slim as she did.

"I'll have the same," Dottie Faye said. "Thanks."

"I'll have the oatmeal and coffee. Thank you." As Emma handed the menu over, she added, "Is Olivia Stewart here? A mutual friend asked me to look her up."

"Olivia's working the cash register right now. Shall I send her over?"

"No, please don't bother," Emma said hastily. "We'll catch her on the way out."

Sarah shrugged. "That's cool. I'll be right back with your coffee."

Emma gazed at the woman behind the cash register. She had wavy red hair pinned up in a bun and a lightly freckled, attractive face. Her demeanor while she checked out customers was pleasant and friendly.

Emma's stomach churned, her slight appetite fleeing. *Have we found Rose's killer at last? Or is this just another wild-goose chase?* Emma and Kelly had traveled across the country and to Europe in search of the students who had attended Rose's last class. One by one they had been cleared through DNA results. Olivia and Danielle Moore were the last two students. Actually, Danielle had been next on the list, but so far they had been unable to find her, despite the help of their detective, Alex Manning. A former New York City policeman, he had access to databases that allowed him to track people beyond their layman's efforts.

Sarah poured coffee into thick white mugs and left again with the promise that their meals would be out shortly.

"I sure hope so," Kelly said, a hand over her midriff. "I'm starving. I would have had breakfast hours ago, but I waited since we were eating out."

"I'm sure it'll be worth it," Dottie Faye said, pouring sugar into her coffee from the glass container. "It smells wonderful in here." It did too, like cinnamon, fresh-baked bread, and bacon. Dottie Faye picked up her spoon and stirred the coffee vigorously.

"Tell me again how you got us this quilt job," Emma said, hoping a change of subject would help calm her nerves.

Dottie Faye waited until she tasted the hot brew before answering. A wide smile flitted across her face. "Bart Tolliver and I go way back. Way, *way* back." She stared into space dreamily.

"How far back?" Kelly prompted. "The ice age?"

Dottie Faye gave a mock pout. "Y'all know I'm not that ancient. Bart says I barely look a day older than when we met." She patted her blond flip into place with a manicured hand.

"Which was when?" Emma rolled her hand in a come-on motion.

"At a college mixer. Bart was attending the University of North Carolina at Chapel Hill. Studying to be a history professor."

"So, he's a Southern gentleman?" Emma asked with a smile. Born and bred in the South, Dottie Faye made no secret of her belief that all things Southern were superior, especially gentlemen.

Before Dottie Faye could answer, Sarah brought their food. The next few minutes were spent spreading jelly on toast made with thick homemade bread, slathering ketchup on home fries, and sprinkling brown sugar on oatmeal.

"Mm, mm, mmmm," Kelly moaned. She scooped another forkful of creamy omelet and crunchy home fries. "This is perfect."

"It sure is," Dottie Faye said, taking a big bite of toast. After swallowing, she continued her story. "Bart is a Yankee. He's lived in Lantern Cove all his life, except for college, of course. His ancestors settled the town." She leaned across the table, lowering her voice. "They were pirates. In fact, most of the town was too."

"I wouldn't have guessed from the poster for Pirate Fest in the window," Kelly said, "and all the pirate decorations in here." The decor included a pirate flag over the wide, brick fireplace, cutlasses crossed over the doorway to the restrooms, and paintings of sailing ships and nefarious-looking seafarers.

"They're definitely embracing their heritage," Emma said. "And from the looks of this restaurant and all the cars in town, it seems to attract tourists." Crowded with patrons, the café vibrated with chatter and the clatter of silverware on dishes, and outside the front plate glass windows, a steady stream of automobiles passed in both directions.

"Salem has witches and Lantern Cove has pirates. Mystic Harbor needs bad guys too," Kelly said. "Fake ones, I mean," she added, noticing Emma's shudder.

"Anyway," Dottie Faye said, "back to Bart. He's decided to open up his house as a museum. His family picked up a bunch of interesting pieces on their voyages around the world—art, furniture, natural history specimens, oddball cultural items, you name it. Plus, he's got an exhibit of relics from his ancestor Benjamin Tolliver's ship, the *Betsy*."

"The museum sounds fascinating," Emma said. "Is the quilt an heirloom?"

"I think so. He said it's from the mid-1800s." Once again, her hand went to her locket. "He gave me this. It belonged to one of his great-grandmothers."

Emma looked at the piece more closely. The circular pendant was gold, enameled with a design in white, gold, red, and blue. "That looks like a compass rose." A compass rose displayed the cardinal directions—North, South, East, and West—as well as intermediate points.

"That's right," Dottie Faye said. "The same design is on the *Betsy*'s logbook and ocean charts."

"A commissioned piece, then," Kelly said. "It's beautiful."

Emma thought of something. "If he's giving you heirloom jewelry, then are you two—"

"Of course not. Why would you think such a thing?" Dottie Faye blushed a color that competed with her generous daubs of rouge.

"Dottie Faye and a Yankee. Wonders will never cease." Kelly shook her head in mock amazement.

"We're friends; that's all." Dottie Faye, while an outrageous flirt, had never been serious about a man since her beloved husband Archibald died decades ago. "I've been helping him with his museum bookkeeping." She waved the locket. "This is just his little old way of saying 'thank you.'"

"If you say so, Dottie Faye." Emma glanced at her watch. "We'd better finish up. Our meeting with your *friend* is in fifteen minutes."

Dottie Faye leisurely spread jelly on her last triangle of toast. "We've got time. His house is just two blocks from here."

A young woman ran into the restaurant from the hallway to the restrooms, tying the sash on her apron as she went. She had bobbed blond hair, a modern style that contrasted oddly with her costume. "Your break was over twenty minutes ago, Mandy," the other waitress said, intercepting her near the coffee station. "Olivia's been asking where you were. And it's not fair to the rest of us. We're slammed."

"I'm so sorry," Mandy said, smoothing her apron into place. "Where do you need me?"

Sarah pointed at the coffee pots. "Do the rounds. Then wait on that new party." A large group was settling themselves near the front, pushing tables together with much scraping.

Mandy brought over the coffee pot and while Emma and Kelly declined, Dottie Faye said, "I'll take half a cup."

"The food was excellent," Emma said kindly while Mandy shakily poured, apparently still upset over being late. "Can you pass that along to the cook?"

She smiled. "I sure will. Josh is his name. He's my boyfriend." She flitted off, and after Sarah brought the check, they went to the cash register to pay.

"How was everything?" Olivia asked as she swiped Dottie Faye's card.

"Great. We'll be back again," Dottie Faye said, signing the slip and adding a generous tip. "We live just up the road."

"Really? Where?"

Despite her friendly smile, Emma noticed a hint of strain around Olivia's pale green eyes. "We're from Mystic Harbor." Emma introduced them and added an invitation for her to stop by Cotton & Grace should she be in town.

"A quilt design shop? That sounds so neat. I used to quilt." She bit her lip, looking like she wanted to say more, but another party pushed their way up to the cash register.

"For once a suspect may come to us." Kelly said when they were outside on the sidewalk.

"That would be nice," Emma said. "But at least we know where to find her." She turned to Dottie Faye. "You want to walk to Bart's house?"

"I think so, Emma Jane. It's just up the street."

"Let me put more money in the meter, then." Emma dug out a few quarters and fed them into the slot in front of her Jeep's parking spot.

The café was on Water Street, which served as the little town's main street. Lined with brick and clapboard storefronts, it had charming cobblestone sidewalks and black hanging lanterns for streetlights. At intervals, little side roads ran down to warehouses and other businesses near the docks. Summer visitors thronged the sidewalks, enjoying the hot and sunny July day as they shopped in the boutiques and gift shops.

Past the business district, the buildings on the left became majestic Federal-style mansions, most with four chimneys, two in the main building and one on each of two wings. Stone steps bordered with metal handrails led up to each house from the sidewalk. Some front yards were delineated with ornate wrought iron fences and many had formal flower gardens and boxwood hedges. Each had a view of the waterfront that had provided their owners' wealth.

"I love these houses," Kelly said. "They're so elegant." She bent to read a brass plaque set on a granite stone post. "Built in 1780. Wow."

"I guess we can figure out where the pirates spent their ill-gotten gains," Emma said wryly. Her cozy house would fit inside one of these three-story behemoths.

Dottie Faye stopped in front of the last mansion on the street. Beyond was a neighborhood of much more modern and modest homes. "Here we are. Number Seven." She climbed the front steps, Emma and Kelly following her to the small semicircular porch supported by white columns. To Emma's surprise, Dottie Faye opened the tall front door and went right in, not bothering to ring the bell or use the anchor-shaped knocker.

"Bart told me he'd leave the door open for us," she explained.

Entering the historic mansion felt like stepping back into history. Breathing the mingled odors of ancient wood and paper and fabric common to old houses, Emma gazed around in admiration. The entrance hall had curved walls, archways, and a sweeping staircase up to the second floor. Richly colored antique rugs covered the stairs as well as the floor, and ornately framed paintings and portraits hung at intervals on the gold-figured wallpaper. The hanging lights and sconces looked like the original gas fixtures.

"Bart? Bart?" Dottie Faye called, hurrying along on her high heels and peering into the long parlors on both sides of the hallway. "He must be upstairs in his office. You girls go ahead and look around, and I'll track him down." She pointed to the room on the left. "The quilt is in there."

The double room, connected by open pocket doors, was crowded with furniture, cabinets, and freestanding pieces. "He's got enough stuff for a museum," Kelly said, edging by a huge stuffed tiger. She gave his moldering head a pat. "Meow."

"Do you see the quilt anywhere?" Emma asked, making her way between a gateleg table holding a silver tea set and a round-fronted cabinet filled with Blue Willow dishes. She bumped the cabinet by accident and everything rattled.

"Nope." Kelly stopped to examine an ebony inlaid Chinese medicine cabinet with dozens of tiny drawers, each trimmed with a carved flower. "This is amazing."

"Focus, Kelly, focus." Emma glimpsed a rectangle of multicolored fabric in a case at the far end of the second room. Was it a tapestry? No, it was behind glass and had a block pattern. It had to be the quilt. "It's back there, Kelly." She found a path through the furniture and Kelly followed.

"This must be very early eighteenth century," Kelly said, viewing the quilt through narrowed, assessing eyes. "It looks similar to one I saw at Colonial Williamsburg."

Emma examined the technique, called inlaid appliqué or intarsia. The twelve-block quilt had a black border on one side with black strips separating the blocks. The appliqué included small portrait figures of men, women, and animals. She sighed deeply. "This job will be a challenge."

"I agree. I don't think we've ever handled such a valuable quilt. In fact, I recommend we conserve rather than restore. It'll maintain its value that way."

"Let's talk to Bart and see what he wants to do. And we'll have to take a closer look first, of course, to decide on the scope and price."

"I wonder if Dottie Faye has found him."

As if in answer, a shriek rent the air, echoing down the staircase and through the high-ceilinged rooms. "Help! Help! Emma. Kelly. Come quick."

Heedless of the antiques, Emma and Kelly turned in one

accord and ran for the stairs. Up and around the steep, winding staircase they went, Emma flying up with ease thanks to her running habit, Kelly moving more slowly. They stopped on the landing. Hallways stretched to the right and left. The staircase to the third floor was straight ahead.

"Dottie Faye?" Emma shouted.

"I'm in here," Dottie Faye called from a partially open door to the right. Emma took off toward it, sneakers pounding on the carpet. Kelly followed close behind.

Emma shoved the door fully open. Dottie Faye stood between a wide mahogany desk and a fireplace, staring down at the floor. "What's wrong, Dottie Faye?"

"He's dead. Oh, Emma! Bart's dead." Dottie Faye grabbed her head with both hands, shaking it back and forth as though negating her words.

They ran to her side, coming to an abrupt halt when they saw the distressing sight. Horror clenched Emma's stomach, and she grabbed Kelly's arm for support.

Bart Tolliver lay face up on the floor, a long silver letter opener protruding from his chest.

two

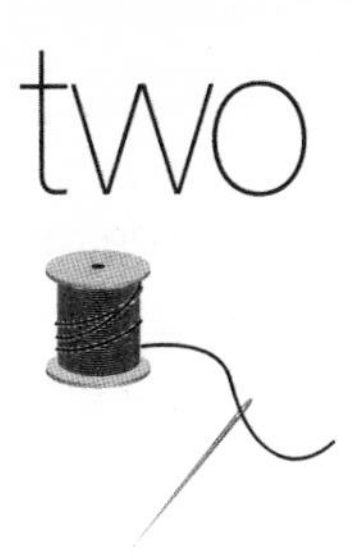

Wresting her eyes from the unfortunate Bart, Emma forced herself to move. She put a hand on her aunt's shoulder. "Come on, Dottie Faye. We need to call the police. We don't want to contaminate the scene any further."

As they stepped back toward the doorway, Emma and Kelly holding Dottie Faye's arms, an older woman entered from the hall. Oddly, she wore garb from the 1800s—a flowing dress, cloak, and bonnet, all in plain navy blue serge. "What's going on?" she snapped, beady dark eyes flashing from face to face. Although petite in height and bone structure, her authoritative bearing made her appear formidably larger.

"Oh, Priscilla—Bart is gone. Your brother is dead," Dottie Faye said, her voice weak and trembling. Emma had never seen her aunt so upset. The absence of her characteristic sassy Southern belle attitude was disturbing. *Had she really cared for this man?*

"He's been stabbed," Emma said. "But I don't recommend—"

Ignoring Emma's warning, Priscilla darted past them to where the body lay. She screamed. Then she flew back to Dottie Faye, fists clenched at her side. "You killed my brother! You ... you ... scheming jezebel!" Apparently her vocabulary was as outdated as her outfit. Priscilla stamped her foot for emphasis, her face filled with rage.

Instinctively, Emma stepped in front of Dottie Faye, blocking the outraged woman from attacking, as it looked like she might. "My aunt didn't kill Bart. We just arrived."

Although we were downstairs a good ten or fifteen minutes before Dottie Faye screamed. She shoved the unwelcome thought aside. "We need to call the police."

"What's this about the police?" A young man appeared in the doorway. Tall and lean, he had reddish-brown hair tied back in a short ponytail. He wore an open flannel shirt over a T-shirt and cargo shorts.

"Nate. Thank goodness you're here. Bart is dead. And these intruders murdered him." Priscilla jabbed a forefinger at the women. "Report them immediately." Reaching for the bow under her chin, she untied the bonnet and pulled it off, revealing a neat head of gray curls.

"Bart's dead? Murdered?" The color drained out of Nate's face. "I can't believe it."

"Stabbed right through the heart." Priscilla's tone held self-righteous relish. She pulled off her cloak next and stashed it with the bonnet on a leather armchair.

"We didn't kill him," Emma said, "and we were just about to call the police."

"I'll do it." Nate's fingers fumbled as he pulled a cellphone from his pocket. He stepped out into the hallway to make the call.

Priscilla beelined back toward the body. "Don't do that, ma'am," Kelly called out. "You'll contaminate the scene." A nasty look flashed across the woman's face. "What do you know about crime scenes?"

Kelly began to explain and Emma took advantage of their argument to pull Dottie Faye out of the room into the hallway. They stood under a stern portrait of Captain Benjamin Tolliver, indicated by a brass plaque. Nate was at the far end of the hall, talking into his phone. "What took you so long to, um, find Bart?" Emma whispered.

Dottie Faye shook her head. "You'll think I'm foolish."

"That's better than the police thinking you guilty."

"I stopped in the powder room to freshen up and ended up doing a full-face makeover."

Emma had seen that process and it did indeed take time. Half the contents of Dottie Faye's handbag were cosmetics.

Dottie Faye's expression brightened. "I can prove it. There are tissues with my lipstick on them in the waste can."

"I'll make sure the police see them."

Nate walked toward them, shoulders slumped. "They'll be right here," he announced. He shook his head. "I still can't believe it."

Kelly had succeeded in calming down Priscilla, and she ushered her through the doorway. "You're in shock, Priscilla," she said gently. "Come sit and rest. Can I get you some tea or a glass of water?"

"I'd like that," Priscilla said. She followed Kelly meekly enough but managed to look daggers at Dottie Faye as they passed by toward the stairs. Emma was reminded of a cat about to hiss and rake its claws over an enemy. "Nate, keep an eye on that woman," Priscilla ordered.

Emma introduced herself and Dottie Faye to Nate. "And you are?" she asked, thinking his features and coloring looked familiar.

"Nate Stewart. I'm Bart's assistant. I'm a doctoral student." Nate brought his hand up to his mouth and held it there a moment as he composed himself. "We were working on a research project," he said quietly, "for my thesis."

"Are you Olivia's brother?" Emma asked, noticing his strong resemblance to the owner of the Crow's Nest Café.

"Why, yes, I am." He raised his brows in inquiry. "You know Olivia?"

"Not exactly," Emma hedged. "We met her today at the Crow's Nest. You two look like brother and sister."

Nate's face sagged in sorrow. "Bart helped Olivia buy the restaurant. He did so much for us." He blinked back tears. "Who could have done this horrible thing?"

"I don't know, Nate. But we'll find out," Dottie Faye said, her voice filled with determination. Nate's distress triggered the return of Dottie Faye's characteristic spunk, Emma noticed with relief.

"I hope so." Sniffing, he wiped his eyes with his plaid sleeve. Sirens, followed by slamming vehicle doors and the pealing of the doorbell, announced the arrival of law enforcement. "I'll go down and let the police in."

"Do you think it was a robbery?" Emma asked Dottie Faye after his footfalls faded. "Maybe Bart interrupted a burglar and he stabbed him. The use of a letter opener seems more spontaneous than planned. Someone should take an inventory of the valuables."

"You could be right, sweet pea." She lowered her voice. "Perhaps I can creep back in there and take a peek, see if anything is missing or out of place."

"Are you sure you're up to doing that?" Emma's eyes searched her aunt's face. "I know you cared for him." She herself wouldn't go back in that office for anything while poor Bart lay there on the carpet.

Dottie Faye's lips trembled. "I want to. For Bart," she managed to say.

"All right. But don't touch anything. Promise?"

Dottie Faye held her hands in the air in demonstration of her obedience to Emma's directive, and then scurried into the office.

Emma stood watch by the door, listening as closely as she

could to what was going on downstairs. She heard the front door open followed by the rumble of men's voices that were soon mingled with Priscilla's shrill tones and Kelly's more moderated voice. "Dottie Faye," she whispered through the doorway, "hurry up. They're coming."

Half a dozen sets of feet tramped back up the staircase. Emma shuffled from foot to foot in agitation. Dottie Faye had better hurry. Being caught for the second time at the crime scene would not look good at all for her aunt.

Dottie Faye sidled back out of the room just as the approaching group reached the top of the stairs. Accompanying Priscilla, Kelly, and Nate were four uniformed officers and a man in a suit. Dottie Faye's eyes glittered with satisfaction as she leaned over and whispered, "You were right, Emma Jane."

But before she could say anything else, Priscilla Tolliver pointed at her. "That's the woman who *discovered* poor Bart."

"Wait out here," the man in the suit ordered. He and two of the officers went inside the office after putting on paper booties and gloves. Within minutes they emerged, the officers taking up guard positions on each side of the door. The suit barked orders into his phone then snapped it shut and shoved it back into the pocket of what Emma realized was a very expensive jacket. He peeled off the gloves. "I'm Detective Spinelli," he said, giving each of them a piercing stare. "The coroner and the crime scene techs are on their way." He handed the discarded gloves to an officer and turned to Priscilla. "Where can I interview people? And I need a place for everyone else to wait."

"Do I have to stay?" Nate asked. "I was," he counted Dottie Faye and the others, "witness number five on the scene." He glanced at his watch. "And I have an appointment in fifteen minutes."

"Cancel it. I want to talk to all of you."

Emma and Kelly exchanged looks. "I'll call Mom," Kelly said, "and tell her we'll be late getting back." To Spinelli, she said, "We own a store in Mystic Harbor." She stepped aside and pulled out her cellphone.

Priscilla opened the next door down the hallway. "This room has a desk and chairs, so it should work for interviews. The rest of us can wait in the kitchen. It's the only suitable place since every other room in the house is stuffed with Bart's collection."

Spinelli peered inside the room, a bedroom from what Emma saw through the partially open doorway. "This will do." He gestured to Dottie Faye. "You were the first on the scene, right? Then let's talk." He pointed to the tallest officer. "Perkins, take the other witnesses downstairs to the kitchen. Get their preliminary information." To another, a Hispanic woman, he said, "Soares, you wait outside for the coroner." Spinelli told another policeman to continue guarding the scene.

Giving Emma and Kelly a beseeching look, Dottie Faye followed Spinelli and an officer into the room.

Perkins and Soares herded the rest of the witnesses downstairs. In the lower hallway, Priscilla said to Soares, "You'll tell people we're closed, right?"

"Yes, ma'am," she said. "I'll be out there until we're through here." She went outside, shutting the door firmly.

"You're already operating as a museum?" Kelly asked Priscilla.

Emma couldn't imagine visitors stumbling through the rooms she and Kelly had entered.

"We've already opened our pirate history exhibit on this side of the house," Priscilla explained, pointing to doorways on their right. "We get a few visitors." She tugged at her skirt. "I'm in character as Benjamin Tolliver's wife, Elizabeth. Benjamin built this house in the 1700s." Turning with a sweep of her dress, she led the group down the hallway into the big, old-fashioned kitchen at the rear of the house.

"Why don't I make tea for everyone?" Kelly offered. Perkins nodded, taking a seat at the long, scrubbed oak table with everyone else.

Kelly went to the six-burner gas stove and turned on the fire under the kettle then dumped the cold contents out of the teapot, rinsed it, and put new bags in.

As everyone sat in glum silence, Emma looked around at the tall cabinets and porcelain sink deep enough to bathe a grown man. The fireplace, like the other she'd seen in the house, was wide and brick. A cast iron cauldron hung from a spit inside the vast space. *This room looks like a museum exhibit too. Not exactly cozy.*

Perkins pulled out a notebook. "While we wait for tea, I'd like to take down your names and contact information." He went around the table, starting with Priscilla.

She lived on a nearby street, Derby Lane, and worked as a docent in the pirate history museum three days a week. Without prompting, she stated that she'd stopped at the bank that morning before coming to work. Priscilla also offered that Nate lived in the Tolliver mansion on the third floor. Bart had employed him to help with Tolliver family research and setting up exhibits. Next he moved on to Emma and Kelly.

The kettle whistled and Kelly poured boiling water into the teapot. As it steeped Emma and Kelly gave Perkins their personal information. Then Emma helped bring mugs to the table. Milk and sugar made the rounds as everyone doctored their tea to their taste.

Emma explained to Perkins why she and Kelly had visited

the mansion that morning and Priscilla perked up. "You restore quilts?" she asked eagerly. "What did you think of ours?"

"It's a very nice piece. I think we can help you," Emma said, hoping this was enough to put her on hold until the police officer was done with his interviews. Apparently, Priscilla wasn't letting her brother's death hamper her plans for the family treasures.

Kelly's brows lifted over her mug, and Emma knew she shared her hope that they could still do the quilt job. In addition to it being an exceptional and rewarding piece to work on, it would give them an excuse to return to the mansion and learn more about Bart's death, if need be—if, for instance, Spinelli considered Dottie Faye a suspect and, God forbid, arrested her. A shiver went down her spine at the thought.

To her relief, a disheveled yet seemingly upbeat Dottie Faye soon entered the kitchen, accompanied by the interviewing officer. He looked at his pad. "Miss Emma Cotton."

Emma scraped back her chair to go to her interview as Dottie Faye headed for the table. "Y'all drinking tea? I'd love some. I'm as dry as a bone." Since Dottie Faye hated tea, this request showed Emma just how upset she was despite her jaunty air.

Upstairs in the interview room, Emma gave Spinelli a detailed account of their morning and the events occurring at the mansion. As she knew he would, he honed in on the time lapse between Dottie Faye going upstairs and when she called out.

Emma squirmed. "Dottie Faye explained that to me. She stopped to do her face. Did you find the tissues in the bathroom?"

Spinelli flicked a glance at the officer taking notes. He didn't answer Emma's question. Instead, he repeated his own. "Tell me again. How long was it between the time your aunt went upstairs and you heard her scream?"

"Ten to fifteen minutes," Emma mumbled.

He made a notation. "Thank you, Miss Cotton. You may go now."

"I think it was a robbery," Emma burst out, not content to end the interview without discussing her theory. Dottie Faye was innocent, no matter what the police thought. "This house is full of valuable items. I think he may have surprised a burglar."

Spinelli's aloof detachment made Emma's blood run cold. "That will be all, Miss Cotton. If we have further questions, we'll contact you."

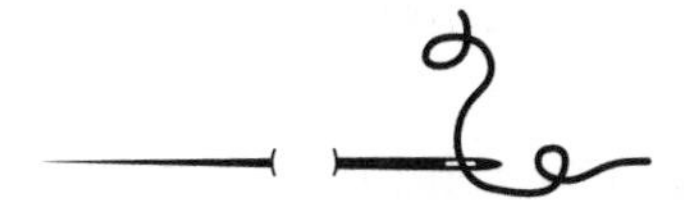

When Kelly's interview was over, the three women were released to go home—Dottie Faye with a warning not to leave Mystic Harbor. As they walked down the hallway toward the front door, Kelly said, "Let's take a peek at the museum before we go."

Dottie Faye opened the door to another double room across from the parlor Emma and Kelly explored earlier. The long expanse was much less cluttered but no less stuffed with interesting items. Around the walls and in glass cases on the floor were artifacts from Benjamin Tolliver's ship, including a female figurehead, the ship's wheel, the sextant, and other navigational aids. There were mannequins of a Revolutionary War soldier, a sea captain, and a pirate with a bandana, eye patch, and pantaloons with a stuffed parrot on his shoulder. Fishing nets draped the ceiling, and the room was lit by the glow of ships' lanterns.

Any items of value were in locked cases, Emma noticed. None looked tampered with. What had the killer wanted? Or was the motive more personal?

"This was Bart's dream," Dottie Faye said, tears glimmering in her eyes. "His way of giving back to the community to relieve his guilt about his family's thieving, treacherous past."

"Maybe Priscilla will carry on," Kelly suggested.

Dottie Faye snorted. "I doubt it. That woman doesn't have an altruistic bone in her body."

"But she's a docent here," Emma pointed out.

"That's so she could keep an eye on her brother, believe me."

Emma thought of something. "What did you notice was missing from the office, Dottie Faye? You didn't have a chance to tell me."

Dottie Faye gestured for them to come closer. "Something big, something even more valuable than anything in this house." She swept her arm to encompass the collection then paused dramatically for such a long time that Emma feared one of the police officers would find them and question why they were still in the house. "You know the project Nate mentioned?"

"Yes, Aunt Dottie. His thesis. Please spit it out." Emma only used "Aunt Dottie"—something Dottie Faye disdained—to let her know that Emma was annoyed by her theatrics.

"He and Bart were on the trail of a hidden treasure. And Bart's map is gone."

three

"Wow. Closing time already," Kelly said, glancing at the store clock. After arriving back in Mystic Harbor from Lantern Cove, they'd had a busy afternoon at the shop. She prepared the bank deposit, gathering cash and checks from the register.

"I'm exhausted," Emma said, heading for the front door to lock it. "It's been a heck of a day." As she flipped the sign to Closed, Dottie Faye suddenly appeared and rapped on the window. Emma opened the door. "What are you doing here? I thought you went home to rest."

Dottie Faye shifted the grocery bag she held to the other hip and walked into the store. "Aren't you going to the special Nimble Thimbles potluck tonight? I had the deli make up my signature chicken salad."

Emma sighed. As much as she loved the Nimble Thimbles, she felt like going home, eating dinner on her porch, and snuggling up with her cat, Ichabod, while she read a book. "I was thinking of skipping the meeting tonight, to be honest."

"I was going to pass on it too, but Mom said she'd bring my contribution, so I guess I'm guilted into it," Kelly said with a laugh as she zipped the deposit into the bank bag.

"You have to go!" Dottie Faye shook her blond locks for emphasis. "Marcia has a special announcement to make."

"Oh, gosh," Emma said. "I hope she's not selling the store." Marcia Goode owned Uncommon Threads, a fabric store.

"No, no. Nothing like that." Dottie's voice was vague. "Get your handbag, sweet pea, and let's head on over."

Emma made one last protest. "I don't have anything to bring. And I don't have time to go to the grocery store." She felt funny about showing up to a potluck empty-handed.

"Don't worry about it, Emma Jane. I ordered a double batch of chicken salad. It's from both of us."

The room above Uncommon Threads was unusually full, and Emma spotted members who rarely attended. Even the youngest member, bubbly teenager Holly Locke, was there, Emma was glad to note. To one side of the room, a long buffet table had been set up. It groaned with a selection of summer salads, soft drinks, iced tea, and plates of baked goodies. As they joined the happy, chattering line in front of the food, Marcia bustled up. "So happy you two could make it." Her round, cheerful face beamed with excitement.

"I'm glad we did too," Emma said, picking up a paper plate. "This all looks fabulous." She served herself a spoonful of the chicken salad, which featured creamy chunks of white meat mixed with grapes and pecans.

"Get your supper, and then I have something important to share." She patted Emma on the arm and hurried off.

"That sounds mysterious," Kelly said. She peered at the contents of a yellow-striped bowl. "Yum. Tokala brought her quinoa salad with butternut squash." She took a heaping portion and put some on Emma's plate. Together they moved along the table, choosing Walter's kale-pecorino dish, Maeve's tossed green salad, and Marcia's egg-potato medley. Maeve had provided freshly baked dinner rolls as Kelly's contribution.

Emma looked at her plate and decided she should skip the brownies. She couldn't resist one of Maeve's rolls, though.

Kelly, as usual, added a brownie and two types of cookies to her mounded plateful. "You want a soda or iced tea?"

"I'll take water." Emma snagged a bottle and tucked it

under her arm, needing both hands to carry her meal to her seat.

The group spent the next half hour eating and catching up with local and personal news. Then, after the last plate had been tossed and the leftovers wrapped, Marcia stood up. "Before we get started on our town history quilt project, I have a special announcement to make."

"And we've all been on pins and needles waiting for it," Walter, the only male member of the group, quipped. Everyone laughed.

"Is that what's been sticking me?" Maeve said, jumping from her chair.

"You're not leaving us, are you?" Tokala asked Marcia, her dark eyes worried.

Marcia shook her head. "No, it's good news. Of course some might consider me leaving to be good news." Everyone laughed again while she put on reading glasses and pulled a folded piece of paper from her pocket. "You all know that I'm a member of the National Preservation Alliance, right? I got involved through the Historical Society when we were redoing the downtown. And without further ado ..." She unfolded the paper and read:

Dear Ms. Goode,

We are pleased to tell you that your nomination of Emma Cotton and Kelly Grace for their work on the Civil War Potholder Quilt has been selected for the top award in our Textiles Category. Congratulations on bringing such a stellar preservation project to our attention.

Emma's heart thumped. She never dreamed her work would receive such prestigious recognition. Highly prized and coveted, the Alliance's awards were the Academy Awards of the conservation and preservation field. The rare potholder quilt, which featured individually quilted and bound blocks joined together, had been stitched by a group of women for a Civil War soldier. Fewer than two dozen of the quilts were known to exist. Emma and Kelly had regarded it as a privilege to work on one.

Kelly put a hand over her heart. "Oh my, Marcia. I can barely breathe. I can't believe it."

Maeve flew to Kelly's side and gave her a kiss on the cheek. "I'm so proud of you, Kelly." She next kissed Emma. "And you, sweetheart."

Not to be outdone, Dottie Faye joined in. "I'm bursting with pride myself. I've always known that my girls were the best in everything they do."

The rest of the group chimed in with congratulations.

"The Alliance will be contacting you soon," Marcia said, taking off her glasses. She handed the letter to Emma. "They'll come in person to present the award."

"You should have a press conference when they do," Tokala suggested. "This is big news for you, your shop, and Mystic Harbor."

"And we should have a party to celebrate," Dottie Faye said, beaming.

"A party? I want to help plan it," Holly Locke said.

"Maybe we can get the quilt back for the award ceremony," Kelly said.

The Massachusetts Heritage Society owned the precious quilt and had commissioned the conservation work.

"That's a great idea," Walter said. "I'm sure the Heritage Society will want to attend."

As everyone took their stations around the Mystic Harbor history quilt they were working on, the discussion turned to planning the event. A vigorous debate was underway about the menu when Emma noticed Dottie Faye had given up on her usual act of pretending to sew and sat slumped back in her seat, staring at her folded hands.

"Are you all right, Dottie Faye?" she whispered.

Her aunt looked up, pain in her big blue eyes. "I'm sorry, sugar pie. I don't want to rain on your parade, but I can't get poor Bart out of my mind."

Maeve, next to her, overheard and gave Dottie Faye's knee a pat. "I don't blame you a bit. Shocking, that was."

Although Maeve and Dottie Faye were often at odds, when the chips were down, they were always supportive of each other.

"What was shocking?" Marcia asked, sympathy flashing across her face.

"Dottie Faye's ... friend ... was found dead today. By poor Dottie Faye herself," Maeve said baldly.

Emma briefly explained to the group what had happened, omitting that the police seemed to suspect Dottie Faye as well as the gruesome details of finding the body.

"Oh my goodness!" Marcia's face was shocked. "What a terrible ordeal for y'all." Like Dottie Faye, Marcia's Southern heritage tended to come out when she was upset.

She got up and gave Dottie Faye a hug.

"Wasn't Bart Tolliver a history professor at the state university?" Walter asked. "I've seen his articles in magazines and newspapers."

"Yes, he was," Dottie Faye said. "He was well known all over the country and often did lecture tours. His family history provided him with most of his material. He even wrote several books about them."

"The Tollivers were privateers, right?" Walter said.

"What's the difference between a pirate and a privateer, except the spelling?" Tokala asked, a skeptical look on her face.

"Privateers were sanctioned by the early Colonial government to capture British ships during the Revolution," Walter explained. "Privateers were used in many other wars, too, including the Civil War."

"Legalized piracy, then," Tokala said.

"They were worse than privateers," Dottie Faye said. "One or two of the less savory limbs of the Tolliver tree were actual pirates in the Caribbean. And all of them smuggled, from the time they settled in the 1600s right up through Prohibition when they brought Canadian whiskey in." She sighed. "The worse thing they did was way, way back when they lured ships onto the rocks just outside the cove."

"That is horrible," Emma said. "No wonder he felt guilty, even if it happened hundreds of years ago."

"They called that wrecking," Kelly said. "I read about that in Daphne du Maurier's novel, *Jamaica Inn*."

"How did you meet Bart, Dottie Faye?" Marcia asked. "At one of his lectures?"

Emma glanced at Dottie Faye in concern, hoping this discussion wasn't upsetting her.

"Oh, no," Dottie Faye said, a dreamy expression on her face. "I met Bart when he was a student, one warm spring night in North Carolina. The azaleas and the dogwoods were in bloom. All of us girls looked so pretty in our party dresses, the men so handsome in their dinner jackets and bow ties. We danced all night. And even though he was a Yankee, he was absolutely charming. And a marvelous dancer." She was silent for a moment. "We dated a few times but then drifted apart. I always had a deep fondness for him, though."

"Did you keep in touch all these years?" Maeve asked. Like the rest of the Nimble Thimbles, she had paused her stitching to hear Dottie Faye's story.

"No. We lost touch that year. But when I was helping Emma Jane and Kelly Ann look for Olivia Stewart, I came across his name. He was presenting a lecture at Hawthorne College, so I went. He remembered me, of course, and after that we saw each other a couple times a week."

Considering Dottie Faye's striking looks and powerful personality, Emma wasn't surprised Bart remembered her, even if he'd last seen her decades ago. "You were helping him with his museum, right?"

"Yes, I was. He had just gotten his nonprofit status and was starting to get donations. He figured that he couldn't change history, but he could use his wealth wisely to educate. Bart was all about education."

"And what about the other part?" Emma asked with a coy smile.

"What other part?"

"Yes, Dottie Faye. You know. The thing Bart was looking for."

"Oh, you mean the treasure."

"Treasure?" Holly squealed, squirming in her seat. "That sounds so cool."

"Hold that thought," Kelly said. "I'm not getting a thing done on this quilt, so I vote we take a break and eat more of those delicious desserts while we listen."

"I'll pass them around," Holly offered, jumping up. She and Kelly made sure everyone who wanted refreshments had something to nibble on or drink.

"Take it away, Dottie Faye," Kelly said, holding a fudgy brownie at the ready.

"Did you know Lantern Cove has a network of tunnels

between the town and the waterfront?" Dottie Faye asked. "That's how they smuggled."

"I didn't know that," Walter said. "But I know Salem does. I went on the tour once. Most of those are blocked up, though."

Some of the other Nimble Thimbles nodded at Walter. Given the short distance between Salem, Massachusetts, and Mystic Harbor, it wasn't surprising that several people in the group knew about the underground tunnels.

"Some of Lantern Cove's aren't, according to Bart. He's been tracking a treasure hidden by Benjamin Tolliver in the tunnels. He planned to donate it to charity."

"I saw Benjamin's portrait at the mansion," Emma put in. "Upstairs near the office."

Dottie Faye nodded. "He was a real a sourpuss, wasn't he? Maybe he had good reason to be since he had a lot of enemies. Anyway, the treasure included jewelry and gold coins—the most famous piece being a gorgeous emerald and diamond necklace Benjamin brought back on one of his voyages." Dottie Faye ran a hand across her neck as though demonstrating the size of the fabled ornament. "Bart believed the treasure was hidden in the tunnels shortly before Benjamin Tolliver was murdered in 1787."

"Was Bart able to find it?" Holly's face was intent with curiosity and excitement.

Dottie Faye's blue eyes shone with satisfaction. "Yes, ma'am. Bart knew the answer was in Benjamin's writings, and he finally figured out the code the old codger used to mark the treasure's location. In our last conversation, he told me he knew exactly where to look, guided by the map."

four

"But you said the map was stolen today." Emma's remark put an end to the group's excited clamor.

"Yes, Emma Jane. The same map."

"The map is gone?" Holly exclaimed.

"Oh, no," Marcia said. "What a shame." Others echoed her dismay.

Dottie Faye smiled smugly, not the reaction Emma was expecting. "Fortunately, I have a copy in a safe place. Bart gave it to me as a backup."

"He must have been worried about someone taking it, then," Emma said. *And he was right. It looked like the treasure was the motive for his murder. Now we just need to convince the police of that.*

"Do you have the cracked code too?" Walter asked. "Maybe you can find the treasure and carry out his wishes."

"I'd love to." Dottie Faye shook her head. "But Bart didn't have a chance to tell me that. Someone came into the room, and he had to hang up. We were going to discuss it today."

"Maybe Nate can help find it," Kelly said. "He was Bart's doctoral student assistant," she explained to the group. "His thesis is research about the treasure."

"Nate might be a suspect," Emma warned. "He may have wanted to keep the treasure for himself. We'll have to tread carefully around him and everyone else connected to Bart."

"How did it go with Olivia Stewart?" Tokala asked.

Emma and Kelly had shared with the group their progress

on Rose's case and the results of trying to find Olivia.

"We met her at the Crow's Nest Café today when we ate breakfast, but we didn't have a chance to talk to her yet," Emma said. "Oddly, I found out that Nate is her brother."

"I wonder if she's involved with Bart's murder?" Walter asked, wiping his hands on a paper napkin and getting up to collect dessert plates from the circle. Holly helped.

Kelly handed Walter her empty paper plate with a nod of thanks. "Nate told us Bart financed her purchase of the restaurant. So, that would be a serious case of biting the hand that feeds you."

"Now you have two murders on your hands," Marcia said. She shook her head. "I hope something breaks soon, on Rose's case, especially. Then you can focus on happier things."

"Like our fantastic award," Kelly said. "How can we ever thank you for nominating us, Marcia?"

"No problem." Marcia waved a dismissive hand. "You two deserve it."

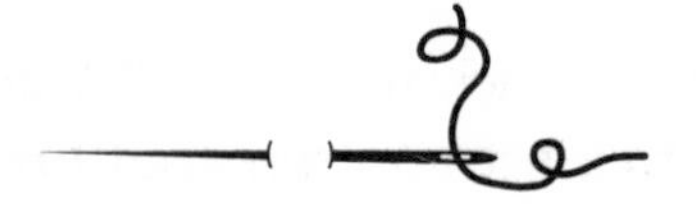

Emma pulled the Jeep into her driveway with a sigh of relief. The day's shocking events had left her drained but wired, a combination that didn't bode well for a restful night. But at least she was home, and just in time too. Thunder rumbled and lightning flickered along the horizon announcing one of the evening thunderstorms common along the coast in hot and humid weather.

As was her habit, she glanced around before getting out of the car, making sure that her door keys were at the ready. Ever since she'd started investigating Rose's death, they had been plagued by mysterious and threatening events that seemed to occur at random. Not seeing anything unusual or out of place, she got out and walked quickly to the front door. The motion detector lights came on, a safety feature she'd installed.

As she inserted the key, she noticed a plain white envelope propped up against the door. She thought it must be a note from her neighbor, Edie Potts, who often communicated that way with a meal invite or a notice regarding something earth-shattering like tree limbs that needed pruning or a Japanese beetle infestation on the peonies. She bent over and scooped it up.

Inside the house, she collected the rest of the mail off the front mat and carried it all into the kitchen. As was his habit, Ichabod dashed out from the bedroom, giving his trademark eerie meow while rubbing against her legs. "Are you hungry?" she asked the little black cat, a stray she had adopted. She put her bag and the mail on the slate countertop and opened the refrigerator to pull out a half-empty tin of canned food. Even though all he did was lick the juice, he made his displeasure known if she didn't give him the smelly treat.

While he lapped eagerly at the fishy dinner, Emma glanced through the postal delivery, reassured to find only bills and junk mail. Although their stalker's threats had been sent to the shop, she always felt a sense of foreboding when reviewing her personal mail. Last was the envelope from Edie.

The flap wasn't sealed and inside was a sheet of folded white paper. Edie must have used a marker because brown spots had bled through to the back.

Unfolding it, she glanced it over.

Shock iced her core and made her hands tremble. Instead of the usual friendly note from Edie, she read, "Blood is red, bruises are blue. Rose is dead. Will you be too?" The brown splotches she'd taken for marker were random reddish splotches. *To resemble blood? Or is it real?*

The letter fell from nerveless fingers, and she stared at it as if it were a poisonous snake. The smart thing to do was preserve it. Unfortunately, her fingerprints were already all over it.

Followed by a curious Ichabod, she hurried to the office for a plastic sleeve. Then, donning a pair of rubber gloves, she picked up the letter and the envelope and slid them inside. She put the sleeve into a manila folder and put it in the file cabinet.

Closing the drawer, she leaned against the cabinet, suddenly even more exhausted. *When will this all be over? Will I ever be free from this sense of impending danger?*

Lightning flashed again, illuminating the wind-tossed trees in the backyard. It was followed immediately by a deafening boom that made Emma jump. Fascinated by the storm, she stood at the office window and watched. After the next clap, the heavens opened up and rain poured down, drumming on the roof.

The storm was so noisy, she felt rather than heard the cellphone in her pocket when it went off. Fearing more bad news, she dug it out with trembling fingers. The display read, "Dr. Eric Hart." Dottie Faye was always trying to convince Emma that the local family doctor was her soul mate. She wasn't sure what Eric thought, but so far she'd managed to keep their relationship at the level of a close friendship.

Sinking down onto the desk chair, she answered, almost yelling to be heard over the rain. Hopefully it would end soon.

"Hello, Emma. Sorry to call so late but I just saw the report on TV. Are you all right?" Eric's voice was warm and soothing, as was his bedside manner.

"The report?" Her stomach lurching, she stood to pace. Had something else happened?

"Bart Tolliver's murder. How terrible for Dottie Faye."

Emma herself hadn't known about the connection between Bart and Dottie Faye until earlier that day. "How did you know Dottie Faye knew Bart?" To hear him better, she walked into the hallway. It was quieter away from the windows.

"They mentioned it on the news. Said she was a person of interest."

A rush of fear and anger swept over Emma. "Who would tell the media that?"

"I don't know. Maybe they made it up." He laughed ruefully. "You know how reporters are."

"Well, she did find his body ... and Kelly and I were there too." The memory of seeing Bart on the floor of his office flooded her mind. She had to force it away by staring at a cheerful watercolor painting of flowers hanging on the wall.

"Oh, my, Emma. That's horrible." He paused. "Is there anything I can do?"

"No, not really. Not right now, anyway."

Eric gave a disgusted snort. "Some friend I am. I've upset you, haven't I?"

She sighed. "Not any more than I already was." She had decided not to mention the threatening letter to Eric. He couldn't do anything, and he'd probably tell her to go to the police. It was a fine idea if she didn't suspect they had been involved in covering up Rose's murder. Instead, she changed the topic to happier news. "At Nimble Thimbles tonight, Kelly and I found out that Marcia nominated us for an award and we got it."

He was gratifyingly excited about the honor and promised to help with the party. The call was winding down, but Eric seemed to have something else on his mind. "Would you happen to be free for lunch sometime this week?" he blurted. "Grounds for Suspicion added some outside tables, and I thought it would be fun to dine alfresco."

Emma had to smile at his use of the Italian term for eating outside. "That does sound nice. Which day works for you?"

They made plans for a couple days later. After saying goodnight, she went into the living room and put on a relaxing music CD before slumping into her comfy chair, noting that the rain had dripped to a stop. What a nightmare it would be if the police decided to arrest Dottie Faye. But surely they didn't suspect her. She had merely been in the wrong place at the wrong time.

Emma shifted restlessly, picking up a cushion and pulling at the fringe. In addition to Bart's death, she felt increasing pressure surrounding their investigation into Rose's murder since they were down to only two suspects. What they would do if neither one matched the female DNA collected by the police from Rose's body didn't bear thinking about. And what could explain the man's DNA?

With a grunt of frustration, she tossed aside the cushion. At this rate, she'd never be able to sleep. *Maybe yoga would help.* After dashing to her bedroom to change into exercise togs, she came back to the room and began a relaxing sequence. Taking deep breaths, she stretched her arms to the ceiling and then moved into a series of poses. Child's pose. Hero. Pigeon. Bow. As she lowered her legs from the Bow, she discovered Ichabod lying right behind her, under her feet. Purring, he walked around to her face, making her laugh.

She picked him up and stroked his head, so much softer now that he had an adequate diet. She'd never guessed how comforting the unconditional love of a pet could be. Snuggling Ichabod made her think of the mysterious prowler again.

While she'd been away in upstate New York, someone had tried to break into her house, and had come back and poisoned Ichabod. A vet had barely been able to save the little feline. And now she had received another threatening letter.

What if the prowler and Rose's killer aren't the same person? Even if the person responsible wasn't guilty of murder, the stalking and harassing activities were illegal.

Who, besides the killer, wants to prevent us from solving the case? Two names immediately came to mind—Ronald Coleman, president of Hawthorne College, and Harry Moran, the former police chief. Both had been instrumental in having Rose's death ruled an accident. *A little too hastily,* Emma thought, *considering that Rose had DNA from two people—one male, one female—under her fingernails.*

She was tired of being afraid, of looking over her shoulder every night, of expecting another unpleasant surprise in the mail or at the shop. It was time to put a stop to the stalker, whoever he or she was.

The beginnings of a plan glimmered in her mind. Perhaps getting a good night's sleep would help bring it into focus.

Picking up Ichabod, she kissed him on his pink nose. "Ready for bed, furry face?"

Perhaps her newfound resolve to take her life back had trickled into her dreams, for Emma's dream about Rose had a decidedly optimistic tone. Yes, she was following her through dark, dank tunnels, but Rose carried an old-fashioned ship's lantern that cast a cheerful gleam. "This way," she called, gesturing for Emma to follow. Up ahead, a glow showed them where the exit was to be found. Even in her sleep, Emma laughed at the literal meaning—a light at the end of the tunnel.

The twittering of birds woke Emma. Feeling refreshed, she went for an early morning run. The streets of Mystic Harbor were quiet, and Emma enjoyed the peace as she ran under lush trees arching overhead, the fragrance of flowers carried on the slight breeze. Although the thunderstorm had refreshed the air, she could tell by the quickly rising temperature that they were in for another scorcher.

She made her usual three-mile loop and headed back to the house, eager to shower and dress for the day. Despite her tired legs, her steps quickened when, with a feeling of foreboding, she spotted Dottie Faye's distinctive white Cadillac convertible parked in front of her house. Even from a distance she could see Dottie Faye's full head of blond hair in the front seat.

Dottie Faye rarely emerged from her house this early in the day.

As she approached the car, the driver door swung open and her aunt climbed out, a little unsteady on her sky-high white sling-backs. "Emma Jane," she cried, "where have you been? I've been waiting forever."

Emma came to halt, bending over with her hands on her knees to catch her breath. She couldn't speak for a moment, breathless from a combination of fatigue and worry.

"I told you that running business was bad for you. Why don't you ever listen to me?" her aunt scolded.

"What is it, Dottie Faye?" Emma gasped out. "What's wrong?"

Dottie Faye's full lips turned down. "The police called. They want me to come in for further questioning. My fingerprints were on the letter opener that killed Bart."

five

"What?" Emma rested her hand on the side of the car for support. "How did your fingerprints get on the letter opener?"

Dottie Faye shrugged. "I used it last week when I helped Bart open donation envelopes." Her voice rose in distress. "I didn't kill him! I swear it upon dear Archibald's grave."

Emma looked around at the neighboring houses, noticing a man emerging to collect his newspaper and a woman walking her dog. Edie Potts twitched her front curtain, ever on alert. Emma wondered if she had seen who left the threatening note. Reminding herself to find out later, she took her aunt's arm. "Let's go inside. We'll figure it out."

Emma made a pot of coffee for Dottie Faye and then took the quickest shower on record. She threw on a T-shirt and jeans and hurried out to the kitchen where Dottie Faye sat morosely at the table watching Ichabod as he observed the birds hopping around the yard, his tail twitching in excitement.

"He's a natural born killer, like all black cats." Dottie Faye's insult about the cat lacked her usual vigor.

"No birds, Ichabod," Emma scolded. "Come on, I'll give you some food."

"Like that's going to work."

The cat trotted over to nibble at his bowl of dry kibble, and after pouring herself a cup of coffee, Emma joined Dottie Faye at the table. "I know you didn't kill Bart, Dottie Faye. But on the surface, I can see why the police might suspect you."

Discovering Bart's body along with fingerprints on the murder weapon didn't exactly add up to a picture of innocence.

"Do you think I need a lawyer?"

Emma debated mentally. The police hated it when a suspect "lawyered up," and it did tend to make someone look guilty. But with this much evidence against Dottie Faye, she needed someone at her side when she talked to the detective. "Yes, I think you should get a defense attorney. This situation is pretty serious to face alone."

"Oh, I want you there, Emma. And Kelly too."

"But we can't go in the interrogation room with you, Dottie Faye. A lawyer can. I'll make some calls."

"No need. I happened to meet the most charming attorney at the country club a couple of weeks ago. Cortland Cabot." Dottie Faye perked up at the mention of him.

"Does he do criminal law?" Emma winced at the sound of that.

Dottie Faye nodded. "I believe so. I have his card in here somewhere." She rooted around in her huge purse, a white one with black polka dots. Pulling out a business card, she read, "Cortland Cabot, Esquire. Criminal Defense Attorney and Counselor-at-Law." She gave a rueful laugh. "I thought I might call him for a dinner party invite. Instead it's as a client. Such an attractive man too." She sighed. "Tall with gray hair and blue eyes."

"You can invite him to dinner after he gets you out of this pickle." *And I'll buy the champagne and party hats*. Of all the scrapes Dottie Faye had managed to get into, this was by far the worst. But to be fair, however, Emma knew she hadn't done anything wrong.

Dottie Faye placed the call while Emma cleaned up their cups and filled Ichabod's water dish.

"He's going to meet me at the police station," Dottie Faye reported. "He doesn't want me to say a peep until he gets there." She got to her feet. "You will come with me, won't you? We can see Olivia again once this ordeal is over."

"That's a thought. Let me call Kelly."

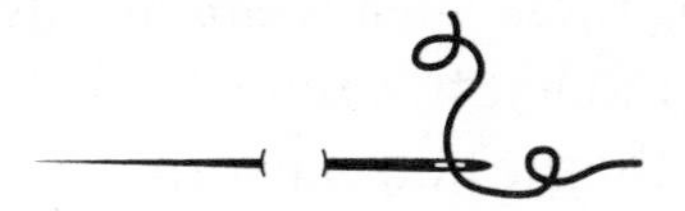

An hour later, Emma and Kelly sat in uncomfortable orange plastic chairs at the Lantern Cove police station waiting for Detective Spinelli to finish questioning Dottie Faye. Maeve was watching the shop again; Emma felt fortunate to have such willing and qualified backup.

"I hope we're done soon," Kelly said, crumpling up a candy wrapper. "I need a real snack. Stale vending machine candy isn't cutting it." She eyed the box of donuts sitting on the front desk.

Emma glanced at the big wall clock behind the protective wire cage that separated the front desk from the waiting area. Dottie Faye and her attorney had been in the back for over an hour. Spinelli's disconcerted face when he saw the urbane, dignified Cortland Cabot in his tailored suit and handmade shoes had been priceless. Dottie Faye had noticed too and sent Emma and Kelly a triumphant smirk as she wiggled her way toward the back of the building. Apparently, Cortland's reputation preceded him.

"I got another threatening letter last night," Emma said, lowering her voice so the desk sergeant wouldn't overhear. She pulled the copy she'd made on her home printer out of her bag and handed it to Kelly.

Kelly stared at the letter in astonishment. "These just keep getting worse. What do you think we should do?"

"I'd like to take the original to Tom Boyer. Maybe later today. I'm sure they won't be able to do anything, but at least it'll be on record."

"The Mystic Harbor police haven't exactly helped us so far."

"I'm not convinced that someone on our list of suspects is the one sending these. I really doubt Olivia ran over to my house last night and left this note. We need to look into the president of Hawthorne and the former police chief."

"You think they might have killed Rose?" Kelly's eyes widened. "I never thought of that."

"Me neither. And no. But they might be behind some of the mysterious events we've been experiencing." Emma ticked them off on her fingers. "Threatening letters and deliveries. Break-ins. Vandalism. Identity theft."

"Or it could be our killer."

"Whoever it is, I'm tired of the harassment. I think we should set a trap."

Kelly rubbed her hands together in glee. "I'm in. This could be fun. How do we begin?"

"I think we need to make an appointment to see President Coleman. As for the retired chief, we should just pop in on him. I've heard he's not the friendliest guy."

They heard the distinctive sound of Dottie Faye's voice approaching and dropped the subject for later. Dottie Faye appeared in good spirits, Emma noted with relief. Cortland Cabot, her attorney, ushered her along gently.

"Don't leave town, Mrs. Sinclair," Spinelli said, following them down the hallway. "We'll be in touch." As the group reached the front desk, he gave Emma and Kelly a curt nod.

Cortland fixed Spinelli with a genteel glare but didn't bother to rise to the bait. "Good day, Detective. You have my number. If you need anything else, call *me*."

Spinelli smirked. "Oh, I'm sure I will. On both counts." He turned smartly and strode away.

"Oh, my. I'm glad that's over," Dottie Faye said, fanning herself with her hand. "Let's go get breakfast at the Crow's Nest. I might be able to keep it down now."

Cortland glanced around. "Let's talk outside."

In the parking lot, standing next to the Cadillac, Cortland turned to Dottie Faye. "Try not to worry, Mrs. Sinclair."

Dottie Faye batted her lashes at the handsome older man. "Please, call me Dottie Faye."

"All right, Dottie Faye." He smiled, a friendly gesture that thawed his otherwise icy and ultra-correct presence. "The evidence isn't all in yet. The medical examiner needs to make his report, and you never know what they'll turn up. The official time of death may even get you off the hook."

"So, you're optimistic?" Emma said. "With the fingerprints—"

"I doubt any crook in the country with television access leaves fingerprints on a murder weapon," Cortland said. "I'm sure Dottie Faye wouldn't have."

"That's for sure. If I was going to kill someone, I'd know better than that." Dottie Faye's voice was vehement.

"They could say it was a crime of passion," Kelly said, a frown creasing her brow.

"Did you two hear any shouting or fighting?" Cortland asked. Both Emma and Kelly shook their heads. "A crime of passion usually needs some kind of buildup. Otherwise, why would your aunt kill someone with two potential witnesses hanging around?"

Those were all good points, and Emma was happy Dottie Faye's attorney was so logical and calm. However, fear still niggled underneath. She'd feel a lot better once this was all cleared up. "If that's all for now, I'll say good day. I'll be in touch." As they chorused goodbyes, Cortland strode off across the lot toward a shiny black BMW SUV.

Kelly opened the door of the Cadillac and pushed the leather seat forward so she could climb in back. "Let's eat."

At the Crow's Nest Café, they were greeted by Mandy, the blond waitress. "Seat yourselves anywhere." She waved at the almost empty room, slow during the late-morning lull before lunch.

"How about that corner booth?" Dottie Faye suggested. The seating in question was semicircular with room for six. Near the windows, it also had the advantage of being isolated.

"That's fine. I'll be right over with water and menus."

The hanging sleigh bells on the door jingled behind them, and Emma turned to see Nate Stewart coming in. Her first thought was that he didn't look well. His shoulders were slumped, and his hair could have used a wash. Her second thought was that it might be easier to get Olivia's attention if Nate were with them.

"Hi, Nate. Would you like to join us?"

His red-rimmed eyes slid over to them, seemingly not having noticed Emma and her companions before she spoke. "Uh, sure."

He shuffled along behind them to the booth and slid in beside Emma who was flanked by Dottie Faye. Kelly slid in from the other side. As he sat down, she noticed a black elastic brace on his left wrist. *Carpel tunnel or an injury?*

"Hey, Nate," Mandy said, passing out menus and glasses of water. "How's it going?" Without waiting for an answer, she asked, "Coffee all around?"

They all ordered coffee, and as Mandy turned to go, Emma asked, "Is Olivia here today?"

"She's in the office. Do you want to see her?"

"Yes. Tell her we're former Hawthorne College students."

"Will do." Mandy briskly strode away, leaving them to debate their meal choices while she fetched their hot beverages.

Emma glanced up from the menu to see Nate watching Mandy, a wistful look on his face. It seemed there might be a history between them.

"They have croissants," Kelly said. "Yum. I think I'll have one with scrambled eggs."

"That sounds delish," Dottie Faye said, setting aside her menu. "But I also want the maple-smoked sausage links."

"Oh, me too."

Mandy reappeared carrying a tray holding coffee mugs and a bowl of creamers. She set them around and put the cream in the middle of the table. "Are you ready to order?" Tucking the tray under her arm, she pulled out a pad and pen. Emma chose poached eggs on wheat and Nate requested homemade donuts, apple cider, and blueberry buttermilk muffins. Upon hearing about those, Kelly added them to her order, "to share."

"The baked goods are really great here," Kelly said. "I loved the bread I had the other day." She added cream and sugar to her coffee and stirred vigorously.

"Yeah, Josh is a good cook." Left unstated but evident in Nate's tone and dismissive expression was a "but" regarding Josh's other attributes. Emma wondered again about the young trio's history.

The swinging door to the kitchen flew open, and Olivia emerged. She glanced around and headed for their booth, giving her brother a little wave.

Her expression as she approached was friendly but puzzled, as if she wondered why they wanted to speak to her. She stopped in front of the table. "I remember you. You ate breakfast here the other day. How can I help you?"

Emma and Kelly exchanged glances. At Kelly's nod, Emma took the lead. "Would you like to join us for a minute? We're former students of Hawthorne College too."

"Don't worry, we're not soliciting donations or anything," Kelly added.

At that, Olivia laughed and slid in next to Kelly. She waved to Mandy, who was walking back toward the kitchen from another table, order pad in hand. "Please bring me a coffee."

Emma rejoiced silently at that. Perhaps they could get her DNA today.

Mandy returned with their meals along with Olivia's coffee, then brought the pot back around for refills. "She's a good waitress," Olivia said, peeling back the cover of an individual creamer, "and her boyfriend, Josh, is a stellar cook. People come from all over to eat here because of him. I was lucky he stayed when I bought the place."

"I'll say," Kelly said. She took a big bite of buttery, flaky croissant. "My compliments to the chef."

"I'll tell him you said that," Olivia said. She frowned. "I can't believe what happened to Bart. I'm just devastated."

Everyone was silent for a moment.

"Bart was such a good man," Nate said. "He helped Olivia buy the café after she moved back from California."

"You used to live in California?" Emma asked, eager to divert the conversation from the murder.

"Yes. San Francisco. I ran a health food restaurant for years. When Nate told me about this opportunity, I moved back. That was about three months ago."

"I love San Francisco," Dottie Faye said. "Chinatown. The fog rising at the Golden Gate Bridge. The street cars."

Olivia snapped her fingers. "I remember you. You're the woman who—"

"Was helping Bart with the museum," Dottie Faye said calmly. She cut a sausage link in half and popped a juicy piece in her mouth. "We had lunch here together last week after we worked on the donations."

"That's right," Olivia said. "I remember Bart telling me he raised several thousand dollars so far."

"But we're not here to talk about Bart," Emma said quickly, eager to forestall further discussion of the murder and Dottie Faye's status as a suspect. "We're looking for your friend Danielle Moore."

"Danielle? What do you want with her?"

"Do you remember Rose Peterson?" Kelly's voice was casual, but her eyes were alert to Olivia's reaction. "She was our best friend." She scooped up a forkful of fluffy eggs.

Olivia's face drained of color, making her pale freckles stand out. "Of course I remember Rose. She was my teacher. She ... um, died." She said to Nate. "She fell down the stairs at school. It was horrible."

She was pushed. And maybe you're responsible. Emma forced the unpleasant thoughts out of her mind so they wouldn't taint her tone and demeanor. "Anyway, we were looking through some things of Rose's recently and we found a project Danielle did. We wanted to return it to her." This was the cover story they'd come up with to find the elusive Danielle.

"Did you try the alumni office?" Olivia took a sip of coffee.

"We did. But they didn't have any information on her, and the Internet was no help either. Another classmate told us you were friends, that you even wore the same necklace."

"Who was that? Gosh, I barely remember anything about that class. It was so long ago."

"Liam Gallagher. He said he had a big crush on you."

Olivia put a hand to her mouth in amazement. "He did? Liam is one person I do remember. He was gorgeous. And I adored his accent. Irish, I think."

"That's where he's living now." Emma didn't mention they had met Liam in person. That would seem a little too much effort for merely returning a project to someone.

"Maybe you could give me his phone number." Her grin let them know that she was joking. She took a deep breath. "You know what, I haven't seen or heard from Danielle since the last night of class. She moved the next day, and I have no idea where. I was kind of hurt by that. I thought we were friends, not just classmates."

Kelly darted an excited glance at Emma. "Did you know of anything that might make her move?"

Olivia shrugged. "Not that I can think of. She did seem tense the last night of class, but that was often the way she was. She was a single mother, and it was hard balancing that and going to school. She was always worried that she would flunk out, even though she studied harder than most of us."

"So, nothing strange happened that last night?" Emma asked.

"Wait a minute. There was something that seemed odd." Olivia paused, appearing to be lost in thought.

Don't stop now. Emma took a sip of her coffee, attempting to conceal her interest.

"She brought this great big book about Swedish Textiles to class and gave it to Rose. The two of them were off whispering about it during our break. When I asked Danielle what was going on, she wouldn't tell me. Rose seemed upset too."

Emma exchanged glances with Kelly. *New information at last.* "That does sound strange."

"Yeah. Why would a book about textiles upset someone?"

Olivia shook her head. "Other than that, everything seemed fine."

"I guess we'll keep looking for Danielle. If you happen to hear from her, would you let us know?"

Kelly produced their business card and handed it to Olivia.

"Sure. But I doubt it. She could be anywhere by now." Olivia waved for Mandy to bring another round of coffee refills.

That's what I'm afraid of—and that we'll never find her or solve the mystery of Rose's death.

Nate groaned in pain in the middle of lifting his coffee cup with his left hand. He winced and set it back down. "I keep forgetting how weak my wrist is."

"What happened to your arm?" Emma asked.

He rubbed the support brace for a few seconds as his lip curled in disgust. "I injured it a while back, and it just won't heal. I might need surgery. Unfortunately, I'm left-handed, so it really messes me up."

"So you have to type one-handed?" Olivia asked. "What a pain. I know you're only partway through your thesis."

"That's another problem." Nate groaned loudly. "With Bart gone, I have no idea where I'm going with that. I might have to start over, and that will set me back six months."

"What is your thesis on?" Emma asked, pretending ignorance of Dottie Faye's disclosure that it was connected to the missing treasure map.

"The topic is actually 'The Role of Smuggling in the Economy of Colonial Massachusetts.' I've built most of my research around Benjamin Tolliver since he was a civic and military leader in addition to making his fortune through privateering and smuggling. He was the mastermind behind the tunnels."

"And you told me the tunnel map is missing, right?" Olivia said.

Nate's face reflected dejection. "Yep. And Bart had just

cracked old Benjamin's clues about where he hid a treasure of jewels and gold coins in the tunnels. Now it's lost forever."

"That must be disappointing," Emma said.

"It is. But it's nothing compared to losing Bart." Swallowing hard, he ducked his head and played with his teaspoon as if unwilling or unable to say more.

"I loved Bart," Olivia said softly. "He was a good friend."

The group sat in silence for a few minutes, everyone lost in their own thoughts.

"It's all my fault," Nate burst out.

Emma felt Dottie Faye jump beside her.

"Hush, Nate. Of course it's not your fault," Olivia said, shaking her head as though to warn him to be quiet.

"I don't mean literally, Livy. But if I'd been there, maybe I could have stopped whoever did it. Obviously they were after the map." At the others' surprised faces, he added. "I noticed it was missing right off. I've been chained to that thing for months."

"Where were you that morning?" Emma asked.

"Out on an errand." Avoiding her gaze, he picked up the spoon and tapped it on the tabletop.

"Well, if we're all done here, I'd better get back to my bookkeeping." Olivia slid out of the booth and stood. She sighed. "With Bart gone, I'm not sure what's going to happen with my loan."

"You mean with the witch in charge?" Nate said with a sour laugh. "And speak of the devil, there she is now."

With a loud jingle of the hanging bells, Priscilla Tolliver pushed through the front door of the diner. Standing with her hands on her hips, she gazed around glaring. Spotting Olivia heading across the room, she started toward her, intercepting her near the door to the kitchen.

Dottie Faye nudged Kelly and nodded toward Olivia's abandoned coffee cup. But just as Kelly reached for it, Mandy swooped it up and put it in a nearby dish bucket.

"Is there anything else I can get you?" she asked. At their headshake, she pulled out the slip and plopped it down in the middle of the table. Then she cleared away their empty plates as they all pretended not to eavesdrop on Olivia and Priscilla's conversation.

"How can I help you, Miss Tolliver?" Olivia asked.

Priscilla continued to crane her neck, staring around at the restaurant. "You and I need to talk, Olivia. I'm in charge here now."

"That wasn't the arrangement I had with your brother," Olivia fired back. "Yes, he loaned me money, but it's my business."

Priscilla smirked. "I guess you didn't read the fine print. He was a co-signer on the purchase agreement, which means I am an owner now. And, there's a clause on the loan paperwork that allows me to escalate the repayment."

"Only if I default," Olivia said. She glanced around at the dozen or so customers. "Can we go somewhere else to discuss this, please?"

Priscilla literally dug her heels in, spreading her legs apart and standing firmly on her wooden-heeled clogs, arms crossed in front of her flat bosom. Although she wasn't in costume today, her long flowing dress was reminiscent of something from the 1800s. "What's wrong with right here?"

"That woman is a piece of work," Kelly whispered, just loud enough for her companions to hear.

Nate shook his head. "You have no idea." He made a swirly motion beside his ear, implying that Priscilla was irrational at best.

Apparently his movement caught Priscilla's eye, for she turned their way. Starting with Nate, her icy gaze swept each in turn. Upon recognizing Dottie Faye, she grew rigid with rage. Clenching both fists, she stormed toward the table.

"You!" She stabbed a finger toward Dottie Faye. Her voice rose to a near-scream, drawing all eyes, including those of a large party just arriving for lunch. "You gold-digging killer!"

SIX

"Excuse me," Dottie Faye said to Kelly. "I'm not going to take this sitting down."

Kelly slid out and Dottie Faye wiggled her way out of the booth. Standing up on her three-inch heels, she was much taller than the diminutive Priscilla. The two of them reminded Emma of a miniature poodle confronting an Afghan hound. But like many small dogs, Priscilla was aggressive out of proportion to her size.

"I'm no gold digger," Dottie Faye said. She snorted. "Bart's fortune is about this big"—she held two fingers an inch apart—"compared to mine."

Hands on her hips, Priscilla thrust her face right up toward Dottie Faye's. "You wanted to marry him and he said no." She sneered. "He never would have married a trailer-trash *belle* like you. The Tollivers come from quality. We're New England royalty."

Dottie Faye's face turned red. "Who are you calling trash? Some royalty. More like scurvy pirates and thieves. At least my fortune was earned honestly."

"By marriage, right?" Priscilla's tone implied Dottie Faye had bartered herself for money.

For a moment, Dottie Faye was speechless, anger, hurt, and humiliation darting across her face. Then her expression hardened into aloof dignity. She shook her head. "I don't know what poor Bart did to deserve a sister as no-account as you. It's a terrible shame that the letter opener didn't find itself a more deserving target."

The meaning of Dottie Faye's words sank in, and Priscilla flew at her, bringing her hand back and slapping Dottie Faye hard on the right cheek. Then she leaped on Dottie Faye, pulled her hair, and wrenched at her blouse.

"No, Miss Tolliver, please!" Olivia ran forward, hands outstretched.

One of the customers shrieked, and another said they should call the police.

Kelly and Emma slid out of the booth, instinctively going to Dottie Faye's defense. But Dottie Faye held her own. She didn't slap back or pull on Priscilla's tight cap of curls. Instead she got one arm around her neck, twisted her around, and brought her to the ground with her superior weight. She sat on Priscilla's back, pinning her down. "Say uncle."

Priscilla thrashed and kicked, swearing. "Get off me, you cow!"

"Not until you promise to calm down."

Sirens chirped, and a police car pulled up in front of the restaurant. Two officers got out, and Emma recognized Soares and Perkins from the murder scene.

"I'm calm. Now let me up."

Emma extended a hand to help Dottie Faye stand. Moving away from Priscilla, Dottie Faye straightened her clothes and patted her hair back into place. Priscilla clambered to her feet with sighs and moans.

"I'm impressed," Kelly said to Dottie Faye, smiling in admiration. "How'd you learn to do that?"

"Didn't I tell you about the time I mud wrestled for charity?" Dottie Faye raised one brow. "It's what us trailer-trash bimbos like to do on a Saturday night."

"Seriously?" Kelly clapped a hand over her mouth to hide her laughter.

"No. I took self-defense lessons at Archibald's insistence. I can take down a person three times her size using a little momentum and leverage," Dottie Faye said as the officers approached.

"What's going on here?" Perkins asked, giving a nod of recognition as he glanced around the circle of faces. The female officer, Soares, pulled out a pad and pen, poised to take notes.

Both Priscilla and Dottie Faye spoke, their voices rising over each other in accusation and recrimination.

Perkins held up his hands. "Hold on. One at a time." He looked at Olivia. "Miss Stewart, since this is your place of business, why don't you tell me what happened."

Olivia stuttered in hesitation. Emma guessed that she was reluctant to blame her new business partner for the disturbance. Nate was still studying his teaspoon, probably equally concerned about implicating Priscilla, who now owned Bart's house, where he was staying.

"I saw the whole thing," interjected a middle-aged woman sitting with three friends in a nearby booth. "That woman"—she pointed at Priscilla—"attacked that woman"—Dottie Faye—"without any provocation whatsoever." She pursed her lips in disgust. "I've never seen such a display. It was like a barroom brawl." Her friends piped up in agreement.

"Why don't you tell me your side of the story," Perkins said to Dottie Faye. With Soares scribbling busily, Dottie Faye led the officers through the sequence of events. Perkins concluded by asking Dottie Faye if she wanted to press charges. Priscilla's eyes almost popped out of her head with rage when she heard that, but she held her tongue.

"No, I don't." Dottie Faye shrugged. "I'm not hurt, just a little embarrassed. When people are upset over losing someone, they can get a little crazy."

"If you're sure, Mrs. Sinclair," Perkins said, "then you're free to go." He turned to Priscilla. "What do you have to say for yourself, Miss Tolliver?"

Priscilla burst into loud sobs. *Another tactic,* Emma thought cynically.

Gesturing to Kelly and Dottie Faye, Emma grabbed the check and headed toward the cash register. As she paid the bill, she heard Priscilla telling the officers that she was distraught over seeing "her brother's killer" in her place of business.

"I guess you're banned from the café," Kelly said to Dottie Faye as they walked out. "At least until Olivia gets Priscilla off her back."

"I'm surprised you didn't press charges," Emma said. "That woman is seriously disturbed."

"Oh, shoot, girls. I got bigger fish to fry." Dottie Faye lowered her voice. "Like figuring out who really killed Bart. And Rose, of course. I haven't forgotten Rose despite this mess, believe me."

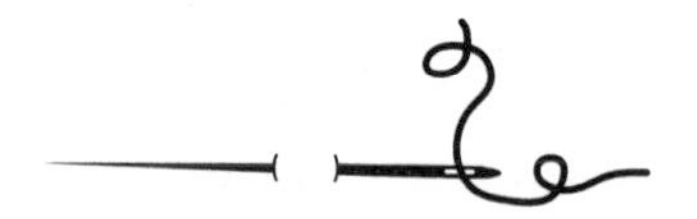

Back in Mystic Harbor, they stopped first at Emma's to get her Jeep and the original copy of the threatening letter. Then Dottie Faye took the Cadillac to the store to join Maeve while Emma and Kelly drove across town to the Mystic Harbor Police Department.

"Two police interactions in one day," Kelly said as she climbed out of the Jeep. "Not exactly my favorite people to spend time with."

As she clicked the car lock, Emma stared at the imposing brick building. The municipal offices were located in a repurposed textile mill with tall, gleaming windows like a row of blind eyes. She hated coming here too. Its grim atmosphere had come to symbolize her painful annual visits to convince Deputy Chief Tom Boyer to reopen Rose's case. So far, he had staunchly refused, continuing to parrot the party line that her death had been an accident. However, someone had sent them the police file, which included the DNA results taken from under Rose's fingernails. Whether the sender had been Boyer or Jack Davis, the retired coroner with a crush on Maeve, was unknown.

Maybe Tom Boyer does want justice, but his hands are tied for some reason. Mine aren't.

Feeling renewed determination, Emma smiled at Kelly. "Ready to beard the lion in his den?"

Inside the station, the officer at the desk recognized Emma. "Here to see the deputy chief, Miss Cotton?" She picked up the phone and buzzed his office.

"Your reputation precedes you," Kelly whispered to Emma.

"Good or bad, I'm sure that's so." Emma held her head high, steeling herself for what was sure to be an unpleasant encounter.

"Hello, Miss Cotton, Mrs. Grace," Tom Boyer said as he sauntered into the waiting area. He made a show of studying the wall calendar. "Your annual visit is early this year." As usual, he had the attitude of someone dealing with a bothersome but unavoidable nuisance.

Undeterred, Emma waved the plastic-clad envelope. "I have something important to show you."

"Come on back." He checked his watch. "I have about five minutes."

Emma and Kelly followed him through the maze of desks leading to his glass-fronted office in the corner. Once inside, Emma pulled the envelope out of the plastic sleeve, took the letter out, and slid them across the desk to Boyer.

"What's this? New evidence?" Brows raised in mockery, he picked up the document by the edges and studied it, front and back. Emma couldn't swear to it, but she thought she saw concern flicker in his hazel eyes before his face shut down, his normal deadpan expression slipping back into place.

"That was delivered to my front door yesterday," Emma said. "It's the latest threat. You can add it to the long list of harassments you have on file for us."

"Obviously you've angered someone," Boyer said, his tone gruff. "Are you still poking around trying to find Rose Peterson's purported killer?"

Emma glanced at Kelly, giving her a slight headshake. There was no way they should tell him about the long list of people they'd investigated. *Or our lack of results to date, unless you counted clearing suspects as a positive outcome.*

"Of course not," Emma lied. "But you know we don't believe it was an accident." She stabbed a finger toward the letter. "This is a direct threat on my life, regardless. What are you going to do about it?"

Boyer sighed. "There's not much I can do. Did you see who delivered it?" He paused. "Thought not. We'll take prints. Maybe we'll get a match." He reached into his drawer and pulled out an evidence bag then slid the letter and envelope into it. "Oh, and be careful."

Kelly, silent until now, walked right up to the desk. "Be careful? Seriously, Boyer. That gem is the sum total of your advice and assistance?" Her mouth turned down in disgust. "Come on, Emma. Let's go."

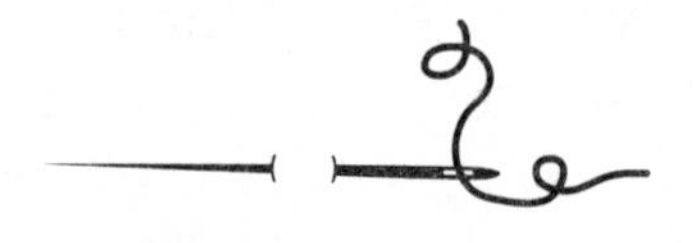

"You've got mail!" Maeve called as Emma and Kelly entered Cotton & Grace a short while later. Smiling broadly, she waved a white envelope.

"Is there a return address?" Emma asked, feeling gun-shy about opening another mysterious letter.

Maeve gave her a strange look. "Of course. It's from New York."

Kelly set the brown paper bag of take-out sandwiches on the counter then grabbed the envelope and ripped it open.

Dottie Faye emerged from among the shelves where she'd been arranging inventory. "Hello, girls. What'd you get us?" She reached into the bag and pulled out paper-wrapped packets. Maeve hurried to the back room to get plates and forks.

"BLTs, pasta salad, and cookies." Kelly quickly scanned the letter. "It's the notification of our award." She gave a whoop, shaking the letter in jubilation, before passing it to Emma.

Emma read the letter, savoring a warm sense of pride and achievement. They did quilt conservation and restoration because they loved it, because they believed in preserving beautiful pieces of fabric art and history for generations to come. Being recognized wasn't necessary or expected, but it really felt good.

She carried the letter to the bulletin board where class and event flyers, photos from customers, and other pertinent documents hung. Finding a spare pushpin, she posted the letter right in the middle where many eyes would see it. "There. What a wonderful honor."

While they munched on the sandwiches made with savory thick bacon, fresh lettuce, and tomatoes, they discussed the back-to-back visits to the police.

"I know what it's like being under suspicion." Maeve shuddered, remembering her own ordeal on their recent trip to Ireland. "It was an experience I don't wish upon anyone."

Kelly gave her mother a hug. "That was one of the worst experiences of my life too."

"At least I've got a good attorney," Dottie Faye said. "And since I'm innocent, I have faith that justice will prevail." She winked at Emma. "And if the police can't help us, I know my girls will uncover the truth."

"Yes we will, or die trying," Emma said, feeling a surge of determination. "I can't believe they consider you a suspect." Innocent people were blamed for murder while real murderers went free. It was maddening.

"And you're close to solving Rose's case too," Dottie Faye said. "I can just feel it."

"Thanks for the vote of confidence, Dottie Faye. I needed it."

"That latest threat means we're getting close, I bet," Kelly said. She dug around in the lunch bag, pulled out the last paper packet, and unwrapped it. "Good. They did have chocolate chip cookies left." She chose a cookie and passed the rest around.

"No, thanks." Emma shook her head. "I can't eat another bite." She put her paper plate into the trash can under the counter. "The only thing we can do is keep moving forward. We'll go back to Lantern Cove and make another attempt at getting Olivia's DNA this week." She pressed a button on the cash register to produce a report of the day's intake so far. "Wow, Maeve. You really racked up the sales."

"I was busy all morning." Maeve said. "And despite this little lull, I predict we'll be busy this afternoon too. A lot of people are in town on vacation."

Emma crumpled the register tape, and it joined the paper plates in the trash. "Back to that threat, I can't believe Olivia or Danielle have been harassing us all this time. Olivia only moved back three months ago. So, I think we have someone else muddying the waters."

"Who would that be?" Maeve asked. Standing beside Emma, she brushed crumbs off the counter and wiped it down with a cloth.

"Maybe the president of the college or the retired chief," Kelly said. She paused to drink from her bottle of water. "Neither of them would listen to us when Rose died, and then the case was classified as an accident. Dr. Jack Davis said they both called and pressured him into ruling it an accident."

"I think we should set a trap for them," Emma said.

"I would love to help," Dottie Faye said. "It'll keep my mind off everything else. What's the plan?"

"I want to visit them both and bait them with a special VIP event." Emma pointed to the letter on the bulletin board. "The preservation award party is the perfect opportunity."

"I'll go see the president," Dottie Faye said. "I'll say I'm going to endow a scholarship." Rising from her perch on a stool, she smoothed her top and grinned smugly. "He'll never refuse to see someone offering to give him money."

"That's probably true," Maeve said. "Maybe you should say the scholarship is in Rose's honor."

Dottie Faye thought that over. "Great idea. Come to think of it, maybe I *will* endow one in her name. Each year, it'll help a deserving textile arts student with their tuition."

As Dottie Faye's words sank in, tears rose to Emma's eyes. "That is one of the sweetest things I've ever heard." She found a tissue in her bag and wiped her nose and eyes.

"Me too," Kelly said. "You're a real peach, Dottie Faye." Her cellphone sent out a sudden jarring tone. "Oh, it's Alex Manning. I'd better grab it." She answered, turning on speakerphone so the rest of them could hear. "Hey, Alex. Got some news for us?"

The detective's brash voice could easily be heard over the

tiny speaker. "I haven't found Danielle yet, if that's what you mean. But I do have some new information."

He paused, forcing Kelly to ask, "And what's that?"

"Danielle checked out a book from the college library and never brought it back."

"So have hundreds of students," Emma said with a laugh.

"Yeah, yeah," Alex said, his tone impatient. "There must have been something special about this book. It was valuable, a 300-page volume called *Impressions in Swedish Textiles*. She checked it out twice during the school year, the second time a few days before Rose's death."

"Olivia mentioned that book," Emma said. "Danielle showed it to Rose the last night of class, and it upset her."

"I wonder if it's related to her death," Kelly said. "I guess we won't know until we find Danielle."

"Did you get Olivia's DNA yet?" Alex asked.

"No, afraid not," Kelly said. "But we're working on it."

"Well, I'm working on finding Danielle. I may have a good lead, finally. It's really strange. It's like she vanished into thin air."

seven

The next morning Emma had something new to feel nervous about—Dr. Eric Hart was taking her to lunch at noon. Pulling her compact out of her handbag, she checked her lip gloss and mascara one more time.

"You look great, Emma," Kelly said, her eyes amused. "I like that pale blue linen shift on you."

"Are you sure you'll be all right here without me? Emma asked, ignoring her friend's comments. "I can cancel if you need me to." Saying yes to Eric had seemed like a good idea at the time, but the closer the date got, the more nervous she felt. Exactly why, she didn't care to examine.

Kelly glanced around at the store, empty except for a couple of browsers. "I think I can handle it." She nodded toward the door. "Besides, Dottie Faye is coming to help. In fact, here she is now."

Emma groaned. She'd managed to keep Dottie Faye from learning about the lunch date. All she needed was her aunt believing that her matchmaking dreams were coming true. Ever since she'd met Eric, Dottie Faye had insisted that he was the man for Emma. She'd been insufferable. And embarrassing.

Dottie Faye, dressed rather formally in a pale pink suit and matching heels for her visit to President Coleman later, stopped short when she spotted Emma. "Why, Emma Jane, you look absolutely lovely today. What's the occasion?"

Kelly threw Emma a mischievous grin. "Someone has a date. With the good doctor, no less."

Emma scowled at her.

With a squeal of delight, Dottie Faye barreled toward her niece.

How can she move that fast on those stiletto heels?

"I see you've finally come to your senses and decided to fulfill your destiny as that adorable man's wife." Reaching her side, she patted Emma's hair into place. "There. You look perfect, sweet pea." Holding Emma's chin, she peered more closely. "Though you could use a little more lipstick."

Emma twisted away. "We've been over this before. Lip gloss is enough for me." Every time she went anywhere near a man, Dottie Faye wanted to doll her up more than she felt comfortable. Maybe for some women makeup was a confidence booster. Emma felt like a fake with too much of it on. It just wasn't her.

Dottie Faye put both hands on her hips. "I just wish you would listen to me for once since I am an expert on the topic of men." She tossed her hair, today flowing around her shoulders, in a Miss America flip. "Makeup brings out your natural beauty by providing a contrast. Your skin is so perfectly pale, like fine porcelain. A darker lipstick would set that off."

"I've got red lipstick, I think," Kelly said, humor glinting in her eyes. She picked up her bag and rooted around.

"I don't think so, Kelly," Emma said, shaking her head. She should have stayed home this morning and told no one about the date. Or better yet, never agreed to it.

"Red isn't the right color for Emma." Dottie Faye searched through her own bag. "I've got a lovely shell pink." She dug out the tube and once again advanced on Emma.

Rather than fight Dottie Faye further, Emma took the lipstick and compact and adorned her lips. Dottie Faye handed her a tissue to blot and stood back. "There. That color will be perfect for your wedding too."

"Wedding?" an amused voice said. Emma turned to see Eric Hart standing there, blond and handsome in casual slacks and polo shirt. "Let me be the first to offer congratulations."

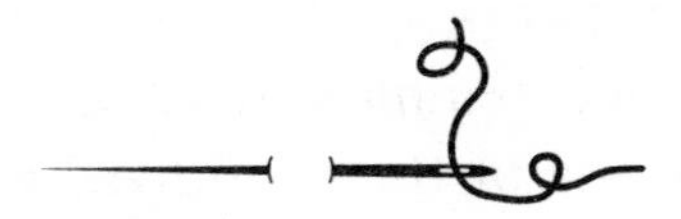

Emma's cheeks were still burning as she and Eric walked along the stone sidewalk to Grounds for Suspicion. "Sorry about that," she said again. "Dottie Faye gets carried away sometimes." *All the time.*

Eric's laugh was a low, pleasant rumble. "She's a romantic. Nothing wrong with that. After all, you'll get married someday, right?"

Emma glanced at Eric in surprise, but his brown eyes were on the sidewalk ahead. In this section of town, roots from the border of ancient maples pushed up through the stones creating a hazard for the unwary walker. She decided to change the subject to something safer. "So, no golf today?" Like many doctors, Eric often took Wednesdays off. Golf was his new passion, and he had the tan to prove it.

"I'll go later, after lunch. With the long days we have this time of year, I can do eighteen holes before sundown." He paused beneath one of the maples. "Riley is at riding camp this week, so I'm not neglecting her."

"I know that," Emma reassured him. The widowed father of a ten-year-old, Eric was as devoted a father as Emma had ever seen. That trait, she realized, was one of his most attractive. "She must love riding camp." Riley adored horses.

"Oh, she's in seventh heaven. I'm afraid she won't want to come home." Eric held open the door of Grounds for Suspicion so she could enter first. Within minutes, they were seated on the new outdoor patio under an umbrella. Around them, other diners laughed and chatted, and the sidewalks beyond were thronged with visitors and townspeople enjoying the perfect summer day.

"This is really nice," Emma said, looking over the familiar menu. She'd had one of their sandwiches just yesterday. Fortunately the offerings were diverse enough she never got bored. The spring mix salad with goat cheese, walnuts, and dried cranberries sounded perfect.

"Isn't it?" Eric studied the menu briefly then put it aside. "I'll have my usual—a turkey Reuben on rye." He laughed and patted his trim stomach. "No fries."

"But you'll work them off playing golf."

"True. I chase more balls into the woods than I drop into the holes." Eric's smile was self-deprecating. "PGA pros are in no danger from me. But I have a good time."

Another appealing trait, Emma realized. A person who laughed at his foibles and flaws was usually pretty well-balanced. She had to admit that the more time she spent with Eric, the more she found to like and admire.

A nervous little thrill ran through her stomach. *Is the 'like' turning into love? And more importantly, am I ready for that?* She pushed the disconcerting thought away. It was a beautiful day, and she was having lunch with a very nice man—a friend. That was all.

The server took their order—Eric did have the fries after all—and during the meal, they kept the discussion on light and pleasant topics. Eric offered again to help with the award celebration, and in turn, Emma asked if he and Riley wanted to join her on a whale-watching cruise later in the month. She'd gotten tickets in a Chamber of Commerce raffle.

Over coffee, Eric asked, his eyes concerned, "How's Dottie

Faye holding up? Has that situation been resolved yet?"

"Not exactly. They brought her in for questioning yesterday. Fortunately she found a lawyer who seems to be on the ball. Cortland Cabot."

Eric whistled. "He's pretty high-powered. Good for her." He snapped his fingers. "One of your suspects lives in Lantern Cove too, doesn't she?"

"Olivia Stewart. Oddly enough, she and Bart Tolliver, the murder victim, were business partners. And get this—Nate Stewart, Olivia's brother—worked for Bart." Emma sighed. "In addition to getting Dottie Faye cleared, I just want to solve Rose's murder and put that whole thing behind me. Get back to a normal life. Besides Olivia, the only suspect remaining is Danielle Moore. Our detective said that she seems to have deliberately disappeared. That makes me think she's guilty."

"Or she's hiding from the person who is," Eric pointed out.

"True. She and Olivia were close friends. Maybe Danielle knows the truth about what happened. Alex thought he had a lead, so I'm hoping he finds her soon."

"I hope so too. I'd like to see you get back to a normal life. Let me know if there's anything I can do. About Rose or Dottie Faye."

"I will, Eric. Thank you." Emma felt warmed by his obvious sincerity. It was nice to know she had a true friend, whether or not their relationship ever went beyond that.

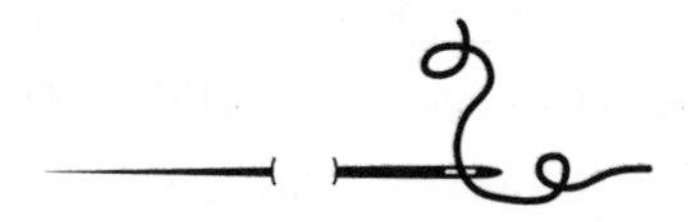

"Can you hear me now?" Dottie Faye asked in a loud whisper.

Emma and Kelly had sneaked into an empty room near

the college president's office so they could be close enough to watch Dottie Faye broadcast over her newest high-tech webcam connected through her cellphone.

"The audio is fine," Emma said. "And the picture is crystal clear."

Indeed, they could plainly see President Coleman's assistant giving Dottie Faye a strange look. The phone buzzed, and the woman picked up the receiver. "President Coleman is ready to see you."

The picture swooped as Dottie Faye bent to retrieve her purse, and then they watched as she walked past the assistant's desk toward Coleman's office.

"This is great," Kelly said to Emma. "It's like being in the room with her."

"Mrs. Sinclair," the assistant announced, standing aside to let Dottie Faye enter the president's spacious and elegantly furnished office.

After a detour to view an eye-catching and valuable Chinese urn, the hidden cam pinned to Dottie Faye's lapel showed President Ronald Coleman, a short, gray-haired man of average build, hurrying to greet his potential donor. In concession to summer temperatures, he wore a lightweight tan gabardine suit and white dress shirt.

"How do you do, Mrs. Sinclair? Please, have a seat." Coleman ushered her to a spot in front of his huge desk. "Would you like a cup of coffee?"

"I'd adore one. Thank you kindly, President Coleman." Dottie Faye's tone was honeyed and very Southern.

"I can tell you hail from south of the Mason-Dixon line," Coleman said as he poured coffee from a carafe into two mugs. "I've spent several vacations sailing off Myrtle Beach with stops in Charleston and Savannah. Lovely historic cities."

"My old stomping grounds," Dottie Faye said. She sighed deeply, as though reminiscing.

"Aren't they all?" Emma murmured. Dottie Faye had a knack of adapting her supposed experience and background to whomever she was buttering up. No human alive could have been all the places or done all the things she claimed.

"Cream or sugar?" Coleman asked.

"Cream and one sugar, please. Were you captain of one of those gorgeous schooners?"

Coleman handed her the cup and scurried around the desk to his own massive leather chair. "No, no. Just a thirty-footer. A friend and I, along with our wives, made up the crew. Jib and mainsail with a motor for backup, of course."

"Of course," Dottie Faye echoed, sounding as if she knew all about it. "It sounds perfectly lovely."

They sipped coffee for a moment before he broke the silence. "I understand you're looking to endow a scholarship. That is such a generous gesture, and we really appreciate it. Many of our students depend on the largesse of donors like yourself."

Dottie Faye gestured widely, setting the camera to bouncing. "The work y'all do here is so vital to our young people. It's the least I can do, to help some deserving student achieve an education. My late husband, Archibald, often expressed his views on the matter." Dottie Faye nattered on a while about Archibald's opinions, Coleman feigning interest much to Emma and Kelly's amusement. Finally she concluded, "My dear niece Emma Cotton and her friend Kelly Grace went to Hawthorne and now they own a local business."

"Is that so?" he asked, getting up and heading to the carafe. "And what might that be?" He brought the carafe to Dottie Faye and topped off her cup.

"Cotton & Grace, a quilt design company. Have you heard of it?"

Coleman sat down again. His face was a study in bewilderment. "Oh, I think I might have wandered in there with my wife a couple of times. It's been a while."

"Liar!" Emma whispered. "He knows exactly who we are."

"You should go again. They've just won an award from the National Preservation Alliance. Highly prestigious."

Was the president's face slightly green, or was it the video quality? No, the video was crystal clear. "Is that so?"

"Yes, indeed." Dottie Faye described the quilt restoration they had done to earn the award. "Why don't you come to the VIP event they're hosting? The mayor and council and every prominent person in Mystic Harbor will be there. You should too."

"Perhaps I will attend, dear lady. Give the date to my assistant, and she can put it on my calendar."

"Yes!" Emma said. "We've got him."

"I'll do that," Dottie Faye said. "And now back to business. I'd like to offer full tuition annually to one deserving student."

Kelly whistled. "Wow. That's amazing."

Coleman gulped. "That is so generous of you, Mrs. Sinclair. Was there a particular department you wanted to focus the scholarship on?"

"Yes, indeed. The Apparel and Textiles Department." Dottie Faye paused dramatically. "I want the scholarship to be an honorarium in the name of Rose Peterson. You know, the poor young woman cut down in her prime right here on campus."

Coleman choked on his coffee and began to cough. Dottie Faye got up and bustled over, still carrying her own cup. She set it on the desk and whacked Coleman on the back.

"I'm ... OK ... just hand me some water, please?" Coleman

pointed to a pitcher of ice water. Dottie Faye poured him a glass. As she handed it to him, she managed to knock over her cup of coffee, which spilled over the desk blotter and dripped down onto Coleman's expensive pant legs. He pushed back violently from the desk with a muffled curse.

"Oh, I'm so sorry," Dottie Faye said, her hands fluttering uselessly about. "Can I get something to wipe it up?"

"Don't worry about it. Excuse me while I clean up." Coleman gently set her aside and hurried out of the office. Dottie Faye pulled a tissue from the box on his desk then used it to grab Coleman's cup.

"What are you doing?" Kelly asked Dottie Faye through their connection.

"You'll see."

Dottie Faye poured the rest of Coleman's coffee into the trash can and then carried the cup back to her seat where she pulled an evidence pouch from her purse. She tucked the DNA sample inside.

eight

To say Dottie Faye was smug as she sashayed into the conference room would be an understatement. "I got that varmint good," she crowed. "Let's get out of here."

Kelly closed her laptop and slid it into its sleeve, then the trio hurriedly clattered down the empty hall to the exit. Outside the president's office, a wiry janitor with a crew cut was arranging cleaning items on his cart. He pulled it over a little to let them by, his beady eyes examining each in turn. "You ladies have a good day now," he said.

"You too, Russ," Dottie Faye said. "Thanks for cleaning up my mess."

"No problem."

In the parking lot, they climbed into the Cadillac. "Why did you take that cup?" Emma asked as Dottie Faye started the engine.

Dottie Faye arranged her big white sunglasses to her satisfaction. "I thought while I was in there, I might as well eliminate—or implicate—President Coleman. Maybe he had a bigger reason than the college's reputation to suppress the truth about Rose." She backed the Caddy out of the parking space.

"That's a good point." Seated in back, Kelly quickly fastened her seat belt. "It can't hurt to check his DNA." She laughed. "I thought he was going to pass out when you mentioned Rose's name."

"He definitely had quite a reaction," Emma said. "And it looked like he wasn't happy when he heard about our award."

"That man sure is a piece of work," Dottie Faye said. "It would be a real pleasure to bring him down a peg or two." She pressed the horn in a jaunty toot of farewell as they exited the parking lot. "I'm sending that cup to the lab today."

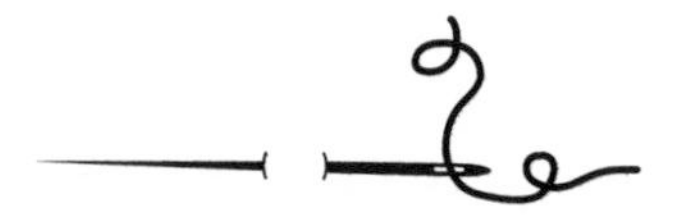

At eight the next morning, Emma was first to arrive at Cotton & Grace. After several stress-filled days, she was looking forward to a boring but peaceful opportunity to catch up with inventory, ordering, and bookwork. Everything tended to fall behind when they were in the thick of an investigation.

But before starting any of those tasks, she stowed her handbag and sat at one of the design desks. Early mornings in the quiet sanctuary of the store were one of Emma's favorite times to mull over ideas for new projects. Today, sunshine streamed through the tall windows, illuminating the colorful inventory and dancing on the hardwood floors. Emma sighed in satisfaction as she pulled out paper and pencil. She adored everything about Cotton & Grace.

What to do? Something summery. Something fresh and fun. Since Mystic Harbor was on the coast, they often created cheerful and colorful nautical-themed bags and other items. Designs depicting sailboats on the bay and beach umbrellas, that kind of thing.

Thinking over the sights and sounds of the past few days, inspiration struck. Working quickly, she sketched a cute design for a beach bag that featured skulls and crossbones, sailing ships, tropical islands, and mermaids. Marcia had some fabrics in stock that would work perfectly.

The doorbell jingled, and Emma looked up to see Kelly bustling into the store, arms laden with bags from the Chocolate Cauldron. "Good morning," Kelly said. "I brought treats. Raspberry chocolate muffins and double lattes." She set everything on the counter and unpacked the goodies.

"Great timing. I just finished a new design idea." Emma brought the sketch over to the counter and showed Kelly.

"Oh, I like that. Customers will too. Everyone loves pirates." Kelly took a sip of her latte. "We could do matching sunglasses cases."

The door jangled again, and Dottie Faye entered carrying a document tube. "Morning, girls." She sniffed at the air. "I smell chocolate."

"I had a feeling you might show up, Dottie Faye, so I bought extra." Kelly pulled another latte out of the bag. "What's in the tube?"

Dottie Faye set it on one of the big worktables and scurried over to take the coffee. "Bart's treasure map," she said nonchalantly, looking over the muffins and selecting one.

Emma's eyes widened. "Really? I want to see that."

"So does Nate. He called me last night, and I invited him to come here this morning before the store opens." Dottie Faye's gaze was innocent. "I didn't think you'd mind. I figured you'd want to hear what he had to say."

There goes my uneventful day. But given a choice of tracking pirate treasure or doing paperwork, the mundane could wait.

"We need to be careful what we say to Nate," Kelly said. "For all we know, he could have killed Bart and stolen the map."

"Why would he want to see my copy then?" Dottie Faye asked, her face troubled as she played with the medallion necklace Bart had given her. "I do like that young man. And Bart thought the world of him."

"Maybe he thinks you have the code," Emma said. "Without it the map is meaningless, right?"

Dottie Faye sighed. "Pretty much. People have been looking for that treasure for more than two hundred years. Hiding it that well was old Benjamin's revenge, I guess."

"I think we should play dumb," Kelly said, "and try to find out as much as we can from Nate. And that means treating him like a suspect for now. Even if he seems to be a nice guy."

"I suppose you're right," Dottie Faye conceded with a frown. Then her face brightened. "Speaking of nice young men, how was your date, Emma Jane?"

Emma flinched. She really didn't want to give a play-by-play of her lunch with Eric. Dottie Faye would parse it for proof that they were a match made in heaven. "It was OK. I had a great salad. Kelly, have you tried the salad with goat cheese?"

"Don't change the topic." Dottie Faye's mouth was set in determination. "Did you have fun?"

"Yes." Emma threw her coffee cup away and picked up the inventory clipboard, hoping that if she looked busy, Dottie Faye would back off.

No such luck. Dottie Faye followed her to the diaper bag display. Not a good choice, considering her aunt's mindset. Dottie Faye fondled a really cute yellow bag with a playful puppy and kitten print, cooing, "I sure wish I could buy one of these for my great-niece or nephew."

Emma grunted and counted the items, making notations. She could feel Dottie Faye's stare, but she resisted saying anything.

Finally, Dottie Faye conceded defeat with a huge sigh. "All right, have it your way, sweet pea. I won't pry anymore. But please, tell me, are you going to see him again?"

Emma considered. She could give her that much, she decided. "We're going to go on a whale watch with Riley. And he's going to help us with the award event."

Dottie Faye clapped her hands. "Good. That's a start, Emma Jane. That's a start."

"Nate's here," Kelly called. She went to greet him at the door.

Emma put away the clipboard and followed Dottie Faye to the worktable. Dottie Faye popped off the end cap and pulled the map out of the tube. "Get me something to weigh down the corners," she instructed as she unrolled the paper. Emma pulled several pattern books from a shelf and arranged them on the map, which was about 24 inches square.

Nate and Kelly joined them at the table. "Ah," Nate said, breathing a long sigh of relief. "I am so thankful Bart thought to give you a copy of the map." He wore his usual outfit consisting of T-shirt, jeans, and open flannel shirt, but he looked a little better, like he'd gotten some rest. And his hair was clean, Emma noticed with relief. She couldn't abide long, greasy hair.

"Why don't you take us through it?" Kelly suggested. "Orient us regarding the town and tunnels."

Nate wasn't wearing his brace today, Emma noticed. "Is your wrist feeling better?"

Using his right hand, he massaged his left wrist. "Yes, thank you. I did something foolish the other day and hurt it. It's all right, if I'm careful." He plucked a fabric marking pen from a nearby carousel of tools. "This map was drawn up just after the American Revolution." Using the pen as a pointer, he indicated the date in the corner, 1784, written in swirling calligraphy. "At that time, the town was quite small, with most of the settlement clustered around the harbor. The Tolliver house was the last on the road leading out of town to the east." He touched the spot with the pen. "Right there."

"I thought the houses past it were much newer," Emma said. "Why are some of the squares marking the buildings red and some yellow?"

Nate showed them the legend in the upper corner. "The red ones are brick, the yellow, wood. The *X* marked through the squares mean barns or other outbuildings. It's great Bart made a color copy; the original map was hand-colored."

"Where are the tunnels?" Dottie Faye asked. "Bart never did have a chance to show me."

"See these dotted lines?" Nate traced one from the waterfront up toward the Tolliver house. It kept going past the house to the next street, Derby Lane.

Emma recognized the street name with a jolt. "Derby Lane is where Priscilla Tolliver lives, isn't it?"

"Sure is." He pointed out a square house. "That's her house. A two-story brick Cape. Not as grand as the Tolliver mansion. It was built for one of the children." He slid the pen along the tunnels, which led from various docks up to buildings in town and also connected east-west along Water Street and several of the parallel streets. "Above ground you can see where the tunnels went by tracing the chimneys. Entrances to the tunnels were built underneath the chimney support arches."

"There was a virtual network," Dottie Faye said. "That's amazing. They could go just about anywhere underground."

Nate laughed. "That's true. And they often did, especially in bad weather or when doing illicit business of one sort or another." He settled back on a stool and folded his arms in a lecturer's stance. "Early in our country's history, the tunnels were used to smuggle in contraband and other spoils. Later, the Tollivers and others used them to evade customs duties. The inspectors would come around and examine their ship's cargos after half the merchandise was spirited away up the tunnels. From there it was moved to stores to be sold. The money was brought to the banks via tunnels, also."

"A real underground economy," Kelly quipped.

"Yes," Nate said. "One that made them extremely wealthy. They brought back treasures from Europe, the Middle East, and the Orient."

"I saw Bart's collection," Emma said. "Some of it looked priceless. Like the quilt he wanted us to restore."

"You're right. Much of it is museum quality." He laughed shortly. "I'm sure Priscilla will be selling it all off to the highest bidder as soon as probate clears."

"If I owned those beautiful family heirlooms," Dottie Faye said, "I'd never let them go."

"That was Bart's goal, as you know, to preserve everything intact. He wanted the house to become a museum that would educate future generations on not just Lantern Cove's history, but Colonial American history." Frowning, he looked down at his sneakers, scuffing one toe across the hardwood floor.

Emma wondered if he had shared Bart's vision. Or had he felt thwarted by it, like Priscilla appeared to be? "So, tell us about the treasure. Why did Bart think it was in the tunnel?"

Nate's face brightened. He unfolded his arms and straightened up. "The story of the treasure was thought to be just a legend for years, one of those rumors that grew with each generation. Benjamin Tolliver was the one who built the family fortune with his voyages to the East. He was also a privateer during the Revolution. Government-sanctioned piracy, we call it. Old Benjamin was a powerful man, said to have the ear of General Washington and our other founding fathers. This, of course, meant he had enemies."

"And that's why he was murdered in 1787," Dottie Faye said. "Right in his own tunnel."

"That's correct," Nate said. He picked up the pen and pointed to the tunnel again. "According to historical accounts, he had been working down on the docks and was going home when he was set upon and stabbed."

Just like his descendent, Bart.

The same thought seemed to strike the others, and they all stood in silence for a few moments.

"So, what about the treasure?" Kelly asked. "How do we even know it existed?"

"Benjamin wrote a letter to his wife, Elizabeth, while at sea telling her he had found, 'an adornment to set off your beauty, reminiscent of the sparkling quality of your lovely eyes.'"

"I take it she had green eyes?" Emma guessed.

"That's right. You can see them in her portrait at the house. However, Elizabeth never received the necklace. She died of pneumonia the day before he returned from sea."

Kelly gasped. "The poor man must have been devastated."

Nate nodded sagely. "He was. Elizabeth lay in state in the front room, as was the custom, and Benjamin placed the necklace around her neck."

"So, maybe it was buried with her?" Emma suggested.

"You might think so. However, the story passed down says the one she wore to her grave was a paste imitation, and Benjamin hid the real one as a bulwark against financial distress. He wasn't quite so romantic as to inter a fortune in jewels. Then he was killed before he could tell anyone where it was."

A sharp rapping came from the front door, and Emma glanced at the wall clock. "Is it time to open already?"

Kelly grabbed her arm. "It's Deputy Chief Boyer. I don't think he's here to buy a tote bag."

nine

Her heart in her throat, Emma hurried to open the door. Did Boyer have news about Rose? Then she saw Detective Spinelli standing behind him.

"Good morning, Emma," Boyer said, his gaze apologetic. "Is your aunt here? She wasn't at home."

This is not good. Her stomach sinking, Emma stood back to let Boyer, Spinelli, and Soares enter the store.

"You must be here for me," Dottie Faye said, moving forward. With amazement, Emma saw that she didn't look the least bit afraid. Dottie Faye held her wrists out dramatically. "Take me now, you misguided scoundrels."

"Dottie Faye Sinclair," Spinelli intoned, frowning, "you are under arrest for the murder of Bart Tolliver."

Soares moved toward Dottie Faye, unclipping a pair of handcuffs from her belt.

"Do you really need to do that?" Emma objected. "She's not going to run away."

"I'm sorry, Emma, but it's policy." Again, Boyer cast Emma a sympathetic look. If she didn't know he was a heartless man, she might think that he cared.

"She's innocent, you know," Kelly protested. "Why are you doing this?"

The officers ignored her.

In another showy move, Dottie Faye stripped off the necklace Bart had given her and held it out to Emma. "Take this for me, sweet pea. I don't want to chance it being *lost* at the station."

Emma took the jewelry and tucked it into her pants pocket, tears pricking at her eyes. She felt so helpless and angry at the sight of her sweet, generous aunt in handcuffs, like a common criminal.

Kelly put an arm around her and squeezed, no doubt thinking of the time Maeve was arrested. "It really stinks, doesn't it?" she murmured. "But it'll be OK. I just know it."

Spinelli read Dottie Faye her rights, and then Soares escorted her toward the door. "Call my attorney," Dottie Faye called back. She tested her wrists against the restraints. "I always wondered what it would be like to be handcuffed."

Soares rolled her eyes. "Come on, Mrs. Sinclair, let's not make this worse than it has to be."

The door slammed behind them. Outside, Soares protected Dottie Faye's head as she slid into the backseat of the Lantern Cove Police cruiser.

"I'm really sorry about your aunt," a voice said behind Emma. She turned to see Nate, looking uncomfortable. "I guess I'd better get going."

Emma nodded. "Our priority right now is getting Dottie Faye out of jail." She shoved her hands into her pockets and felt the hard pendant of the necklace. Pulling it out, she noticed that it had a little seam and catch. It was a locket. She popped it open and saw a tiny piece of paper inside: "The seventh step in the seventh gate." *What the heck?*

Nate moved closer. "Did you find something?" His voice was eager as he craned his neck to see inside the necklace's compartment.

Acting on instinct, Emma snapped the locket shut and slid it back into her pocket. "Nope. Just a love note from Bart to Dottie Faye. It's private."

Nate shrugged and ambled forward, heading for the door.

Then he stopped. "It'd be awesome if you could get me a copy of the map. I'll pay for it."

"I'll have to ask Dottie Faye. It belongs to her."

"OK, then. See you later." He slipped through the front door and walked down the sidewalk.

"I have to call Cortland," Emma said. She hurried to the counter and searched for the phone book with trembling hands. "Oh, why didn't I get one of his cards?"

Kelly's thumbs worked the screen of her smartphone. "I've got it." She hit the button to dial and held the phone out to Emma. "Unless you want me to talk to him?"

Emma shook her head and took the phone. "I'll do it." She explained the situation to the receptionist and was reassured that Dottie Faye was a priority. "He's going to call this number back once he knows what's going on," she said, handing the phone back to Kelly. She went to a display of tote bags and pulled everything down from the shelves.

"What are you doing?"

Emma began to arrange the bags by size and color. "I need to keep busy." When life got hectic and confusing, she found comfort in being able to order her physical environment, as foolish as that might have seemed to others.

Kelly pressed icons on her phone. "I'm going to ask Mom to come in. You might have to go to Lantern Cove."

"Thanks." Emma slotted several bags on the shelf, tweaking them into place.

"She'll be right down," Kelly said, setting her phone on the counter next to the cash register. "By the way, what was in that locket? I didn't believe your story about a love note for a second. Dottie Faye would probably frame one of those, not hide it away."

Emma laughed. "You're right. I'm sure it was a clue to the

treasure. I just didn't want Nate to know that."

"Really? Can I see it?" Kelly hurried to Emma's side.

Emma fished the locket out of her pocket and handed it to Kelly. "We should put that in our safe. The map, too, if it fits. We might have to fold it up." After several disasters at the store, they had invested in a small, fireproof safe for their valuable papers, extra checks, and computer backups. Hidden in a closet under some storage tubs, it was bolted to the floor.

"Seventh step in the seventh gate,'" Kelly mused. "I wonder what that means." She closed the locket and carried it back to the table, and then folded the map.

"I have no idea. Maybe Dottie Faye does." Emma moved on to the next shelf, a row of quilted wallet covers and sunglasses cases. "I hope Cortland calls soon."

"Me too," Kelly said, her voice muffled as she opened the safe in the closet.

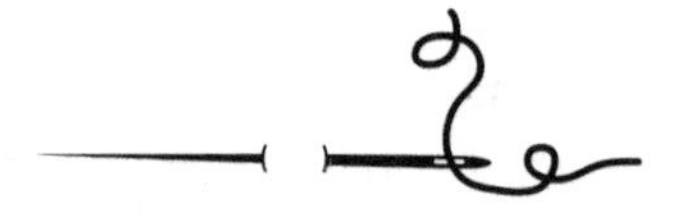

"Good morning, girls." Maeve bustled into the store in her usual energetic way. She wore a cheerful summer outfit consisting of a pale green blouse and matching capris that set off her hair and eyes. "I got here as soon as I could." She tucked her bag under the counter and logged onto the cash register.

"We really appreciate it, Maeve," Emma said. "We're just waiting for Dottie Faye's lawyer to call."

Kelly's phone jangled. "There he is now," Kelly said, looking at the display.

Emma snatched it up. Kelly and her mother watched anxiously as Emma listened to the attorney. After she hung up, she glanced at the clock. "I do have to leave. Cortland got Dottie Faye a bond hearing on the docket this morning. I can make it if I hurry."

"Go with her, Kelly," Maeve urged. At Kelly's protest at leaving her alone, she flapped her hand. "I'll be fine. Emma needs you right now."

"Thanks so much, Mom." Kelly pulled her car keys out of her bag. "Let's go, Emma. I'm driving." As an afterthought, she grabbed the sack holding the remaining muffins. "In case we get hungry on the road."

Although Emma loved to drive her Jeep, she appreciated not having to concentrate on traffic while she was so worried about Dottie Faye. Anxiety and distress gnawed at her stomach, making her feel like she was in a bad dream. After experiencing Rose's unsolved murder, she didn't have much faith in the justice meted out by the system. The fact that Dottie Faye had been arrested at all was ludicrous, in her view.

Kelly, seeming to sense Emma's need to be alone with her thoughts, drove in silence to Lantern Cove, where she found the last parking space near the courthouse. After pushing a handful of quarters into the meter, they hurried into the old brick building and up the wide marble staircase to the second-floor courtroom. The big door opened with a hushed swing, and they found seats in the row closest to the front where Dottie Faye and Cortland sat at the defendant's table. She shot them a tiny wave and smile.

"All rise," the bailiff said. They obeyed, and the judge emerged from a door behind the bench. He was an older man, bald, short, and with thick glasses. He sat at the bench and hit the gavel. "Court is now in session." They went through the court procedures, and then the judge read the charges. "Dottie Faye Sinclair, you are charged with murder in the second degree in the death of Bartholomew Benjamin Tolliver."

Emma knew that meant that the murder wasn't premeditated but neither was it accidental.

"How do you plead?"

"Not guilty, your Honor," Cortland said.

"I'm innocent," Dottie Faye blurted.

Cortland tugged on Dottie Faye's sleeve, indicating she should hush up. Then he made a case for granting Dottie Faye bond based on the circumstantial nature of the evidence.

The prosecutor, a shifty-looking, ginger-haired man with buckteeth, objected. "Mrs. Sinclair is a woman of means. She'll flee the country."

"She'll surrender her passport to the court," Cortland countered. "Mrs. Sinclair has no criminal record and is an upstanding citizen who donates generously to charity. Her only living relative is in Mystic Harbor, where she resides." Dottie Faye shot another glance at Emma, as though to underline Cortland's statement.

"In light of the circumstances and Mrs. Sinclair's age"—Emma was sure she heard an insulted snort from the defendant—"bond is granted in the amount of $250,000." The judge banged his gavel.

Relief surged through Emma. Dottie Faye was free—for now—and that gave them time to find out who really killed Bart. Dottie Faye turned and gave them the two-fisted victory shake before leaving the courtroom to be officially released.

In the hallway, Cortland intercepted them. "I'd be happy to give Dottie Faye a ride back to Mystic Harbor. It'll take a while to get the bond paperwork processed, and she needs to get her belongings from the police station."

"That would be great," Emma said. "Tell her to call me once she's settled." She shook the attorney's warm, strong hand. "Thank you so much for all you've done. I'm so glad she doesn't have to stay in jail until the next proceeding."

Cortland set his square jaw, blue eyes darkening in determination. "Jail is no place for a fine woman like Dottie Faye. And if I have my way, she won't spend another moment there." He nodded goodbye.

"He's the kind of lawyer to have," Kelly said, watching Cortland stride down the hallway with authority.

"That's for sure. I feel much better about the situation with him involved." Emma glanced at her watch and walked toward the stairs. "I suppose we'd better get back to the store."

"I have a better idea. Our route takes us past Echo Pond."

"What did you have in mind? Taking a dip?"

"Not exactly. Retired Chief Harry Moran lives there."

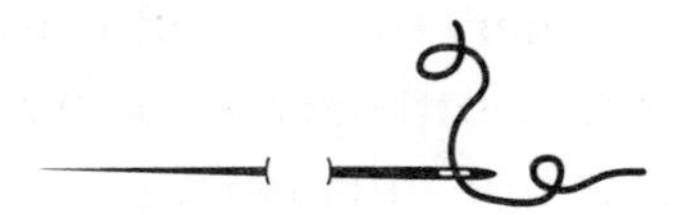

On the outskirts of Mystic Harbor, Echo Pond was surrounded by cabins, some winterized for year-round residency. Not large enough to allow speedboats, the pond had escaped the mini-mansion syndrome, retaining a quiet stillness favored by fisherman and kayakers. Harry Moran owned one of the year-round houses, a small, white clapboard ranch with green trim. The tiny square of neglected lawn in front held only a mailbox and a sawing lumberjack whirligig set in motion by the breeze.

"It looks like he's home," Emma said, noticing an old pickup truck in the short driveway. There wasn't room behind it for the Honda SUV, so they parked on the side of the dirt road.

No one answered their knocking on the front door.

"Maybe he isn't home." Emma amended her earlier

assumption that the retiree rarely went anywhere.

"I bet he's down on the pond," Kelly said. "Let's go see." She led the way around the side of the house and down a short, steep slope to the shorefront. Like the others along the water, the property had a dock extending into the pond. While they watched, a man at the helm of a small fishing boat headed their way, the trolling motor buzzing.

He cut the motor and brought the boat to a gliding stop as they reached the dock. Frowning up at them, he barked, "Help you with something?" Under a billed cap, his eyes were cold, warning them off. Reaching out, he hitched the boat to a cleat.

Kelly was undaunted by his gruff manner. "Chief Moran, I presume?"

He grunted. "Former chief." Bending over, he organized his gear, opening and shutting cases with a clatter of latches.

"I'm Kelly Grace and this is Emma Cotton. We own a business in town."

Moran swabbed the bottom of the boat with a sponge, squeezed it overboard, and tossed it back into a coffee can.

"Good day fishing?" Emma asked in an attempt to engage the man.

"Nope. Nothing was biting." Without looking at them, he set the tackle cases on the dock and clambered out of the boat.

Kelly and Emma backed up a little but held their ground. "We're here to talk to you about Rose Peterson," Kelly said.

He paused in the middle of retrieving his fishing pole from the boat. "Who?" Despite his professed ignorance, Emma sensed his tension.

"Rose Peterson," Kelly said again. "The young woman who was murdered at Hawthorne College fifteen years ago."

Moran chuckled. "Oh, her. Now I remember. You mean

fell down the stairs." Still clutching the pole, he picked up the tackle cases and plodded up the dock toward them. "You'll have to excuse me. I've got a busy schedule this afternoon."

A flare of anger burned away the intimidation Emma felt at Moran's hostility. "Busy tying fishing flies? Come on, Chief Moran. Rose's death was no accident, like you claim."

Moran stopped dead and glared at them. "What are you two doing messing with a police investigation? And a closed one to boot."

"An investigation that was closed too soon. DNA evidence shows two people fought with Rose that night," Kelly said.

"How do you know that?" he snapped. His face reddened when he realized his slip. Dropping his fishing gear, he advanced on them, shaking his fist. "Go on, get out of here before I have you arrested for trespassing."

"Good grief. We just wanted to talk to you," Kelly said.

"Some things are better left alone. I'd be real careful if I were you."

ten

"Is that a threat?" Emma's blood was boiling. "I wonder what Deputy Chief Boyer would think of that." Standing with arms folded across her chest and legs firmly planted, she returned glare for glare. She was sick of cowering in the shadows like a victim.

Moran was the first to break eye contact. Like many bullies, he was actually weak when confronted. "Listen, I didn't mean anything. I just don't want you slandering me."

"You mean discussing what a good job you did investigating Rose's death? If you're content with your efforts, why worry about what's said?"

His mouth dropped open and he stuttered, not able to answer her logic.

"Come on, Emma, let's go," Kelly said. "We aren't going to get any help here."

"You're right, Kelly." Emma sent one last scowl Moran's way before turning to walk up the hill. She felt his eyes on them most of the way, but when she turned back at the corner of the house, she saw him pacing back and forth talking on a cellphone.

Out of his sight, they broke into a trot and jumped into the SUV. Kelly started the engine with a roar and pulled out so fast, gravel spun under the tires.

A wave of relieved hysteria bubbled in Emma's chest. Now that the confrontation was over, she felt both jazzed and exhausted. "What a horrible, horrible man."

"He sure is," Kelly agreed, peering into the rearview to make sure the irate Moran wasn't following them. "If our intent was to poke a snake into striking, I think we succeeded."

"Yeah, if he isn't the prowler, he'll probably become one." Emma's eyes met Kelly and they both giggled. "Tell you what, Kelly, once this case is over, I'm hanging up my detective badge permanently."

"Me too." Kelly's agreement was fervent. Spotting a fast-food restaurant, she slowed the SUV and put on her turn signal. "I don't know about you, but I'm starved." She sent Emma a grin. "And yes, I want fries with that."

Back at the shop, they found Dottie Faye working behind the counter with Maeve.

Emma went right over to Dottie Faye and gave her a big hug. "I thought you'd go home and rest after your ordeal."

"Shoot, no. I'm all cranked up. Nothing like being falsely accused to light a fire under your—" Dottie Faye smiled at a customer laden with merchandise. "Are you ready to check out?" As the woman unloaded her basket, Dottie Faye asked Emma, "Do you have my necklace?"

"It's in the safe. I'll get it for you." Emma walked toward the back.

Kelly followed. "Let's call Alex and have him look into our Lantern Cove friends."

"Good idea." Emma went to the closet and removed Dottie Faye's necklace from the safe. "Let me give this to Dottie Faye, and then let's go upstairs to talk to him privately."

Above the store was a little apartment used for storage and the occasional guest, like Kelly's sister Kathleen who came and left town at irregular intervals. Kelly dialed Alex and put him on speakerphone.

"Hello, ladies," he said, his voice muffled. "Sorry. You

caught me eating lunch." The crackling of paper and a loud crunch followed.

Kelly rolled her eyes at Emma. "That's OK. As long as you can take notes. We want you to look into a few people for us."

Crunch. Crunch. "You mean you uncovered some new suspects? I thought Danielle was it."

"This is for a different case," Emma said. "Dottie Faye has been arrested for murder."

Dead silence was followed by an audible gulp as he swallowed. "What?"

Emma quickly filled him in. "We know Dottie Faye is innocent, so we'd like some background on the other people involved. You might find something to help point us in the right direction regarding a motive."

"Oh, if it exists, I'll find it." Lack of confidence was not the detective's problem. "Who are these clowns?"

Emma gave him the list. "Bartholomew Tolliver, age 70, was the victim. Priscilla Tolliver is a little younger; she's his sister. And Nate Stewart worked for Bart. He's a doctoral student at the university. He's about—what, Kelly? Thirty or so?"

"That sounds right."

"Stewart as in Olivia?"

"Yes. She's Nate's older sister," Kelly said.

"Interesting."

"It is," Emma added, "especially since Bart helped finance Olivia's purchase of the restaurant."

"How does Bart's death affect that?"

"It doesn't help her if that's what you mean," Emma said. "Priscilla is Bart's heir, so now Olivia has to deal with her."

"And from our experience, that is not a good thing," Kelly said.

"All right then. If that's it, I'll look into them this

afternoon. Later." With a final crackle of paper, he hung up.

"He's something else." Kelly shook her head in bemusement.

"As long as he gets the info, I don't care how strange he is." Emma stared into space, thinking. "Before we go back downstairs, I'd like to make another call. To Tom Boyer."

For once the deputy chief took her call immediately. "Good afternoon, Miss Cotton. How can I help you?"

"Good afternoon to you too, Deputy Chief. I have a couple of things to discuss. I've got you on speakerphone. Kelly Grace is with me."

"Hello, Mrs. Grace. Go ahead. Tell me what's up."

Emma started with the easy topic. "Did you find any fingerprints on that note I brought you?"

Boyer's voice held a note of regret. "I'm afraid not. But I wasn't really expecting to find any. Most people know better nowadays and wear gloves."

Emma felt a pang of disappointment. That would have been too easy. "Oh, well. I'm not surprised." She paused, thinking best how to approach the next item of discussion. Finally, she decided to just spit it out. "Did you hear from Harry Moran today? You know, the retired chief."

"Uh, no." Boyer's voice rose in irritation. "What did you do this time?"

Why did this man always make her feel like a scolded child? Emma glanced at Kelly, who gave her an encouraging nod before pointing at herself to indicate she would take the heat. Emma shook her head. Maybe one of them could stay on the good side of the local law. "We stopped by his house today to ask him about Rose Peterson. And he ended up threatening us."

Boyer scoffed. "I highly doubt that. Moran is an old curmudgeon, but he doesn't go around threatening people."

Emma looked at Kelly again for reinforcement. "Kelly heard it too. He said, and I quote, 'Some things are better left alone. I'd be careful if I were you.' What does that sound like to you?"

Boyer was silent for a moment. "Sounds like an irritated retiree. Maybe he thought you were criticizing his police work."

Emma grimaced at Kelly. "Yeah, that's what he tried to imply." She sighed. Why did she bother? Boyer was never going to believe them until another serious crime was committed or they found irrefutable proof about Rose's death. She hoped for the latter. She made her tone crisp and businesslike. "I won't take any more of your time. I've done my duty and reported the incident. What happens next is on your head."

Boyer changed tack, injecting an ultra-reasonable, almost paternal note into his voice. "I wish I could convince you that it's best for you and everyone if you drop your fruitless quest into Rose's death. It's understandable. I know you cared about her. But you can't go around accusing people of dereliction of duty."

Emma bit her lip until she got her unruly emotions under control. "We didn't do that. He's the one who flew off the handle." She huffed loudly. "Sorry to bother you, Deputy Chief. Goodbye." She pushed the icon on Kelly's phone to cut him off. "That man makes me so mad." Clenching her fists at her sides, she paced back and forth in the small room.

"We never believed he'd really do anything anyway. If he hasn't over the last fifteen years, why would he now?"

Emma stopped in front of the window, staring down at the sunlit street. "You're right. We did our duty and told him about it. That's all we can do, I guess." She noticed a gaggle of shoppers coming down the sidewalk toward Cotton &

Grace. "We'd better get down there and help your mom and Dottie Faye before they disown us."

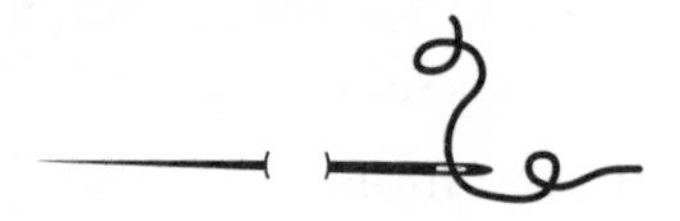

"This was a great idea," Emma said, stretching back in a lounge chair on Kelly's spacious deck. She accepted a tall, frosty glass of iced tea from Kelly with a contented sigh. Patrick turned sizzling chicken breasts on the grill, and the deck dining table was laid with salads and other meal accouterments. In the garden, Maeve and Dottie Faye strolled along viewing the lush perennial beds filled with day lilies, daisies, and delphiniums. There really was nothing more relaxing than a cookout with friends on a beautiful and hot summer night.

Kelly took the adjacent chair. "We had a very productive day at the store despite court this morning and our visit to Moran. I feel like we're finally getting caught up."

"Once you finalize June's books, I'll be able to get the quarterly financials done for you," Patrick said, closing the grill lid and seating himself nearby. As always when he grilled, he wore an apron that read, "I cook more than the books." His accounting practice prepared the taxes and financial statements for Cotton & Grace. Kelly and Emma kept a check register and sales information at the store, and they also did the banking.

"I have a feeling we're up this year," Emma said. "The inventory is just flying off the shelves. And we've had some big commissions for restorations."

Dottie Faye, followed by Maeve, came up the deck steps. "I was thinking, Emma Jane ..." She paused to pull out a seat from the big round table. Maeve sat beside her.

"Not again, Dottie Faye," Kelly said, adding a fake groan.

"Shoot. I know you're just teasing me. Where would you be without my brainstorms?"

"Go ahead, Dottie Faye," Emma said. "What were you thinking?"

"You should call Miss Priscilla and arrange to do that quilt job. Not only will it mean a fat check, it will also get you inside the crime scene. Then you two can do some investigating and help me clear my name." She picked up her glass of tea and took a sip. "You made this sweet tea just right, Maeve."

"Well, after a few years of nagging, I guess I learned." Maeve's smile belied her words. She and Dottie Faye had often crossed swords, but over time they had become friends.

Emma was still thinking about what Dottie Faye had suggested. "That's not a bad idea. I'd love to get my hands on that quilt." For Patrick and Maeve's benefit, she explained the rarity of the intarsia style.

Patrick hopped up to pull the chicken breasts off the grill. "It sounds like a good plan. But get paid up front, in case Priscilla is guilty. You don't want to do all that work for nothing." Using a big fork, he put the chicken on a platter.

"Spoken like a true accountant," Kelly said, getting up from her lounge chair and moving to the table. "Everyone, help yourself."

They all passed around the platter of meat and bowls of potato, three-bean, and tossed green salad. Once plates were heaped, they dug in.

"This is a lot better than prison food," Dottie Faye said, waving her fork. "Uh-huh. That's for sure."

Emma almost choked on a bite of chicken. "Dottie Faye! You weren't in there long enough to eat anything."

"Just sayin'," her aunt replied, unperturbed.

"I love this potato salad," Patrick said, scooping up another big forkful. "What'd you put in it, Dottie Faye?"

"It's an old Southern recipe I got from my grandma. It's got mayonnaise, celery salt, sweet onion, and dill pickles. If you make it warm and then chill it in the icebox, the flavors sink in."

"I'll have to try that." Patrick genuinely liked to cook and often made dinner when Kelly was working late at the store or was out of town. In return, she took over meal duty during tax season when Patrick worked twelve-hour days.

Emma's cellphone shrilled, interrupting the feast. She looked at it dancing in the seat of her lounge chair. "I'll just let it go to voice mail."

It continued to ring. "Maybe it's important," Dottie Faye said. She widened her eyes. "Maybe it's Eric."

"I'm not certain those two are the same."

"Yeah, they are," Kelly said with a smirk.

Rolling her eyes, Emma put down her napkin and got up. "I'll answer it, and then turn it off."

She glanced at the caller ID. *Unknown. Hmm.* "Hello?" she said, peeved at being interrupted by what was undoubtedly a sales call.

The caller didn't say anything. But as Emma listened, she heard the distinct sound of heavy breathing.

eleven

"Hello?" Emma said again.

The breathing stopped and there was a hollow silence. Then a robotic-sounding voice said, "Blood is red ..." Just like the note. Emma didn't wait to hear more. She disconnected and threw the phone down on to the chair, recoiling as if it were a poisonous insect.

Kelly pushed back her chair in alarm and stood. "Emma! What's wrong?"

Emma put a shaking hand to her mouth. "It was another threat. He ... she ... whoever it was started quoting that letter to me."

"What letter?" Dottie Faye asked.

That was right. Only Kelly knew about the letter. Emma explained how she'd come home to find the envelope and that, of course, the police hadn't found fingerprints. "Obviously this was the same person."

"Or someone who read it," Kelly said. "Besides me, since I'm sitting right here."

Emma had to smile at her friend's joke. "As if."

"What did the voice sound like?" Patrick asked.

Emma thought back. "It sounded strange, electronic almost. I couldn't really tell if it was male or female."

"No doubt that's what they intended," Maeve said. "He probably used some kind of computer program to alter his voice."

Emma sat back down at the table. "Sorry, everyone. I

didn't mean to ruin dinner." She picked up her fork and made a pretense of eating.

"This person sounds like they're getting really nasty," Patrick said. "Maybe you two should drop the investigation."

Emma felt a pang. Despite the fear, distress, and worry caused by the threats, she was more determined than ever to solve the mystery of Rose's death. "You could be right, Patrick, and I don't blame you for being concerned. But I've gone too far to stop now." She looked at Kelly. "If you want to quit, I totally understand. You have children."

Kelly shook her head vigorously. "No way. I'm going to see this through until the end. Rose was my friend too." She shot a loving look at her husband. "We'll be careful, Patrick. Promise."

"I have to admit I'm glad. I couldn't have gotten this far without you. Or you, Dottie Faye." Frankly, Emma was relieved that Kelly was going to continue helping with the case. Their very different traits and abilities seem to meld into a harmonious whole while investigating, just as they did at Cotton & Grace. And without Dottie Faye's assistance, both financial and otherwise, they never would have gotten out of the gate.

"Wouldn't miss it for the world, sweet pea," Dottie Faye said. "I'm glad I'm in a position to help."

"Well, now that's settled, who wants strawberry shortcake with real whipped cream?" Maeve got up from the table. "And I'll put a pot of decaf on."

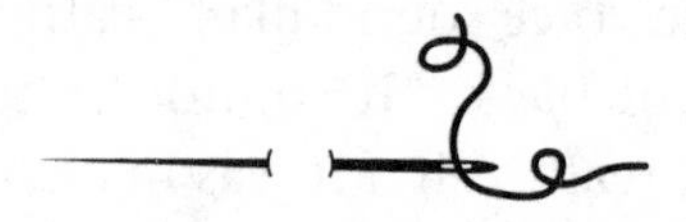

Alex called with an update as they drove to Lantern Cove in Emma's Jeep late the next morning. Priscilla had been more than happy to have them evaluate the quilt once they mentioned its rarity and value. They had to promise her that Dottie Faye would not be with them, however.

Kelly put Alex on speaker as usual. "Hey, Alex. Do you have anything for us?"

"You bet. I never give up until I get answers. I'm stubborn that way. I should know Danielle Moore's location in a day or so. I'm just checking out a couple more things."

Emma felt a rush of relief. She'd been worried they would never find Danielle. It was a big world out there. People could and did disappear, never to be heard from again. "That's great news, Alex. Thanks."

"Yes, great news," Kelly echoed. "So, did you get anything on our Lantern Cove friends yet?"

"Friends?" Alex sounded puzzled. The detective tended to be literal and often lacked a sense of humor.

Kelly made a face at the phone. "Just a figure of speech. Suspects. Except for the man who was killed, of course."

"Yes, as a matter of fact I did. OK, then. Here we go." Alex was apparently scanning his computer screen or printed reports. "Nathaniel Dexter Stewart. Age thirty-one. No police record. Has a few parking tickets in Boston." Alex laughed. "He'd better clear those up before his car gets booted. And he owes over a hundred grand in student loans." He whistled. "Sure would hate to have that debt hanging around my neck. Especially for degrees in history." He snickered.

Emma glanced over at Kelly. "Sounds like a possible motive."

"What was that?" Alex asked.

"Nothing," Kelly said. "How about Priscilla? Anything on her?"

"Let me see. Yes. Sixty-eight years old. Owns a house on Derby Lane in Lantern Cove. No income except her deceased husband's estate, which appears to have been hard hit during the last recession."

"She used her maiden name for everything?" Emma asked.

"Looks that way. Her husband, Silas Wolcott, was a banker in Lantern Cove."

"Great info, Alex. Anything on the victim, Bart Tolliver?"

"Yep." There was silence for a moment. "Hang on. It's right here." Then they heard a humming sound. "Bart was pretty well-fixed. Good investments. Put quite a chunk into starting up that nonprofit museum. The only donor last year, when he set it up."

"So everything looks OK with that?"

"Far as I can tell. You might want to ask an accountant to check over the paperwork."

"I'll have my husband look into it," Kelly said. "Thanks again, Alex."

"Yes, thanks. Call us right away when you find Danielle."

Emma turned off the main road and headed into the village of Lantern Cove, winding past historic houses into the waterfront area. She had to slow to a crawl to edge through the throngs of tourists milling about the streets. Tents and rides set up in the town square off Water Street announced the start of Pirate Fest.

"Maybe we should have a Mystic Harbor summer fest," Kelly said. "They're certainly getting a lot of visitors."

Emma noticed a man on a street corner dressed in pirate garb and brandishing his fake sword to the amusement of children nearby. "We need a theme. Salem has witches. Lantern Cove has pirates."

"I think we should do a heritage crafts festival. Quilting, knitting, lace-making, stitching. We can include painting and other visual arts."

"That's a great idea. Maybe we can take the proposal to the Chamber of Commerce." Emma sighed. "After we're done solving these cases."

Despite the crowds, they found a spot in front of Bart's house and Emma parallel parked along the granite curb. Most tourists didn't venture as far as the residential section. As they got out and Emma locked the car, faint sounds of carnival music could be heard from the town square.

Like the other nearby houses, the Tolliver mansion drowsed in the shade under venerable maple trees almost as old as the house. Emma felt a shiver of unease. How could something as horrific as Bart's murder happen here, in this decorous, historic neighborhood?

Kelly must have been thinking along the same lines. "It's hard to believe that such a picturesque place has such a bloodthirsty history," she said as they climbed the stairs from the street. "And apparently it's not a thing of the past."

"Unfortunately not. I hope we'll be able to learn something to help Dottie Faye today. I wish I had a clue about what to look for." Emma tried the front door. It was locked, and she noticed a sign taped to the wood saying that the museum was "closed indefinitely." Emma rang the bell. No answer. "She did say to meet her here, right?"

"She sure did." Kelly put her face to the sidelight and peered inside then rapped on the glass. "Here she comes."

Emma heard the click of deadbolts being turned and then the massive door creaked open. When Priscilla saw who it was, she pasted a smile on her face, a grimace that reminded Emma of a stuffed alligator she'd once seen. The woman had the weathered complexion and sly malevolence characteristic of the reptile species. Today she wore a powder blue pantsuit instead of an old-fashioned costume.

"Come in, come in." Priscilla pulled the door farther open to let them enter.

"Good morning, Miss Tolliver," Emma said. "Thanks again for inviting us to look at that lovely quilt."

"You'll be able to give me an estimate today?" She cocked her head, scrutinizing Emma and Kelly from head to toe as though their appearance might give clues to their competence. "Can you tell me what needs to be done as well as the value?"

Kelly showed her the tote bag that held their supplies. "We'll certainly give you a preliminary value. An appraiser will have to be consulted for a final determination."

"I've got one coming later this morning."

She's moving fast. Bart isn't even buried yet. As far as Emma knew, the medical examiner hadn't released his body.

Priscilla slammed the front door and set the deadbolts. "I have to lock it or else all kinds of people wander in. They think the museum is still open even though I put up a sign. But that's tourists for you." She shook her gray curls in disbelief as she led the way into the room where the quilt was displayed. "I didn't touch the quilt, like you said. I just left it where it was."

"Bart was wise to store it in a glass case out of direct sunlight," Emma said as she put on thin white gloves. Kelly did the same. "We've seen valuable quilts nailed to a wall."

"Anything can discolor antique textiles." Kelly opened the tote bag and pulled out a cotton drop cloth and laid it on the carpet. "Nails, tacks, wood, regular paper, plastic, newsprint ... the list goes on."

Priscilla shuddered. "Worrying about such things is too much work for me. I can't wait to get rid of it all."

If this gorgeous quilt were mine, I'd never let it go. Emma paused to admire the intricate stitching and design of the antique piece before opening the front drop panel of the case. With Kelly's help, she shifted the quilt to the drop cloth, treating it as if it were as fragile as the mounted butterflies in a nearby case. She knew from unfortunate experience that even a slight tug or pull could shred delicate fabrics.

"You said you had a bed we could lay this on?" Emma preferred a table, but the only large one available was in the kitchen, and there was no way she would bring this quilt in there and chance soiling.

"Upstairs. I'll show you."

"Great. Do you mind bringing our bag?" Emma picked up one end of the sling they'd made for the quilt. Kelly took the other.

With a grumble, Priscilla complied, picking up the tote and leading them upstairs. The bedroom was to the left of the stairs and faced the back of the house. Sunlight streamed through two tall windows, illuminating the four-poster pineapple bed and matching armoire, bureau, and night tables.

"We'll need the curtains closed," Emma said as she and Kelly placed the quilt on the bed. She quickly pulled the thick drapes across one window while Priscilla did the same with the other. Kelly turned on a lamp.

Then, working together, they laid the quilt and cloth out on the bed, gently smoothing the quilt into place while Priscilla watched.

"One of my great-greats put that together in the early 1700s," Priscilla said. "She brought it with her when she came from England to marry a Tolliver."

"It's a beautiful piece," Emma said. "I've only seen work this old in museums. The figurative design is especially rare." Very few early quilts depicting human figures had survived.

"My ancestors never threw anything away."

"That's fortunate," Kelly said.

"It is if you don't have to deal with it." She grunted. "The attics are stuffed with junk."

Emma glanced at Kelly, and judging by the glint in her eyes, she guessed she shared her bemusement regarding Priscilla's attitude.

Emma pulled out a measuring tape and magnifying glass from the tote, and Kelly placed acid-free paper and a pencil on top of the bureau. Emma would examine the quilt while Kelly made notes as to condition and damage. Then they'd swap roles to confirm each other's work.

"Measures 71 inches long by 63 inches wide," Emma said as she measured the quilt without touching the tape to the surface.

Kelly noted the numbers on a diagram she had sketched.

Emma bent closer and examined the fabric through the magnifying glass. "The fabric is silk and velvet. Some metallic thread, but the piecing and basting threads appear to be linen and silk. The backing is linen." She ran her gloved hand reverently over the quilt, thinking of the woman who had stitched it centuries ago. For Emma, textile arts of all vintages had an intrinsic value endowed by their tangible connection to a legacy of women who had created beauty with their hands.

As Emma moved on to examine each block of the quilt, Priscilla continued to watch them with eagle eyes. Emma wished she would find something else to do. She hated having people watch her work, but she didn't want to risk alienating her difficult client by suggesting she leave them alone. When Nate Stewart called Priscilla's name from the hallway, she felt a sense of relief.

"I wonder what he wants," Priscilla grumbled. She moved toward the door, but Nate pushed it open and stuck his head into the room.

"There you are, Miss Tolliver. I've been looking all over

the house for you." He gave the others a wave of greeting and a brief smile.

Priscilla gestured toward the bed. "I'm busy, as you can see. What can I help you with?"

"We need to talk. As I told you, my standing in my degree program is in jeopardy unless I can finish my research."

The older woman shrugged. "That's too bad." She glanced at Emma and Kelly still performing their examination while pretending not to listen. "Let's step out in the hallway."

She and Nate moved out of the room but Emma could still hear them clearly through the partly open door.

"As I told you, Nate, you can't stay here anymore. I'm getting ready to sell the house."

"I suppose I can move out, but I still need access to Bart's papers and books. I'm at a critical point in my research into the family history." Nate sounded almost desperate. Was the research really for his doctoral thesis or was he hoping to find the clue to the treasure?

"That's not my problem. I don't care a fig about the family history or having people poke their noses into it. It's no one's business."

"If everyone thought that way, we'd have no history books or education," Kelly murmured just loud enough for Emma to hear.

"Please, Miss Tolliver, I just need another two months, and I'll be out of your hair. You won't be ready to sell before that, will you? There's tons of stuff in this house to deal with. And I know what most of it is and what it's worth. I won't let you be cheated."

She was silent. Whether Priscilla was considering his predicament or making him suffer, Emma wasn't sure. She guessed the latter.

"I can help you pack the place up if you want. Do some painting, repairs, whatever you need."

Emma wondered how he'd be able to do all that with an injured wrist.

"All right," Priscilla finally said, a grudging note in her voice. "If you help me, I'll let you stay. But just until we get the house cleaned out and listed." The doorbell rang. "That must be the appraiser." Footsteps thudding on the carpet, they moved down the hall toward the stairs. "But get one thing straight, young man. No one's going to cheat me. I'm not the foolish old lady everyone thinks I am."

Kelly dashed to the door and closed it all the way, deadening the sound of Nate's abject assurances. "Whew. What an old battle-ax."

"Hey, that's our client you're talking about," Emma joked. "But you're right. Poor Nate. I felt embarrassed for him, having to beg like that." Standing up straight, she put one hand to her lower back and rubbed it with her knuckles. "This bed is a little too low." She pulled off her gloves and set them on the nightstand.

"Let's take a break. She'll be busy for a while with the appraiser. His eyes are going to pop out when he sees all the antiques and collectibles downstairs." Kelly took off her gloves too and ran her hand along the satiny top of the bureau. "I love mahogany."

"They probably brought the wood from the West Indies," Emma said, admiring the bedroom set's dark glossy finish. The pineapple motif on the bedposts was echoed in the carved columns running down the sides of the other pieces. In addition, the armoire had a carved, arched crest with a pineapple in the center.

"Pineapples everywhere," Kelly said with a laugh. "I

wonder if Priscilla realizes they're a sign of hospitality?"

"She probably didn't get that memo." Acting on a whim, Emma pulled on the armoire door's handle. Slightly swollen due to humidity, it took quite a tug to get it open.

"Emma!" Kelly scolded, but she hurried over to peek at the contents.

Tight-packed clothing hung inside, emitting a scent of mothballs and dusty old wool and cotton.

"These clothes are all vintage," Emma said, holding up a sprigged cotton dress with a scooped neck and lace-trimmed sleeves. It had to date from the late 1800s. "Now I know where Priscilla gets her costumes. She's actually small enough to fit into them." With a rueful smile, she demonstrated the tiny waist of the dress, meant to be worn with a tight-laced corset.

"I'll say." Kelly giggled at a man's tailcoat. "Can you see Patrick wearing something like this?" She pulled a top hat down from the shelf above and popped it onto her head. "With this of course."

"Too funny." Emma pushed the clothes along the rod, looking at each piece. Then something out of place caught her eye. Balled up on the floor behind a pair of high-buttoned shoes was what looked like a modern man's flannel shirt.

Her pulse raced as she bent down and picked it up. Instead of feeling soft and flexible, it was oddly stiff. What were those rusty red patches all over it?

Emma dropped the shirt to the carpet as she realized the answer. The plaid shirt was stained with blood.

twelve

Kelly stared at the shirt in horror. "Is that what I think it is?"

"Blood? I think so." Emma nudged it with the toe of her sneaker. "See how the red stains are all down the front? I'll bet the murderer wore this when he or she killed Bart." A picture flashed into her mind of someone wearing the shirt and stabbing Bart. A messy death, to be sure, and it appeared the shirt had taken the brunt of it.

"It looks like one of those shirts Nate wears." Kelly hunkered down and peered at the label. "Men's large. That looks about right. He and Patrick look about the same size and that's what he wears."

"The killer must have stashed it here. But where did he go? Did he hide somewhere? Both Priscilla and Nate arrived after we got here. Or so they said." She considered the bed—the space underneath was too tight for a fully grown human. So was the overstuffed armoire. The room had no closet. Yet the killer had stopped to bury the shirt in the armoire. So, he or she had been in this room at some point. Maybe it was put here at a later time. *But why?*

"We'll have to think about that. Right now we should find a different place to hide this evidence. The killer might dispose of it. I'm surprised they didn't already."

"You realize that would be considered tampering with evidence?" Emma pointed out.

"Yes, but I think it's worth the risk. Otherwise it's going

to disappear, I just know it. We'll put it back later, right before we inform the police it's here."

Emma wasn't totally convinced, but when she heard voices outside the door, she decided to take a chance. Anything to help Dottie Faye. "Uh-oh. They're coming. Where should we put it?" She dashed to the bureau and opened drawers. "How about in here? They just have bed linens in them."

Kelly shook her head. "Too obvious." Kneeling down, she flipped up the white tufted chenille bedspread. "Let's put it in between the box spring and the mattress. No one will look there." She held the mattresses up while Emma stuffed the shirt in between as far as she could reach, scrunching her face up in distaste as she tried to avoid touching the stained sections.

Kelly straightened the spread, and they stood up just as the doorknob rattled.

They were back at their stations, gloves on, magnifier and pencil in hand, by the time the door swung open. Priscilla entered, followed by a short, slight man wearing khakis and a short-sleeved shirt, and carrying a computer tablet. A digital camera was slung around his neck.

"Emma, Kelly, I'd like you to meet Sam Bates. He's doing the appraisal for me." Priscilla's demeanor had totally changed. She actually appeared pleasant and agreeable.

"Nice to meet you. To be exact, I'm going to be leading the team." Sam gazed around the room in admiration. "There are too many items of fine quality for just one person to do it all. I'll be pulling together art, furniture, and collectibles experts. Today I'm just jotting down notes on the highlights."

"Cotton & Grace is working on an estimate for this quilt,"

Priscilla said, pointing toward the bed. "But they told me a more formal appraisal will be needed."

"I'd like to take a look, if I may," Sam said. He set his tablet on the bureau, and then took off his camera and placed it beside the tablet. Reaching into his pocket, he pulled out a pair of cotton gloves much like the ones Emma and Kelly wore.

"I see you're prepared," Kelly said with a smile.

"I never travel without my gloves. You never know when you'll come across a fine antique—oh my. This is exquisite." Sam peered more closely at the quilt, and then held out his hand for the magnifying glass. Emma placed it in his palm. "Intarsia, if I'm not mistaken. I haven't seen anything of this caliber outside the Smithsonian."

"That's right," Emma said. "I told Miss Tolliver that it's extremely rare."

Sam stood up and tapped the magnifying glass against his palm. "What are you planning to do to it? I did spot quite a lot of damage. Which, of course, is expected in textiles of that vintage."

The appraiser's eyes regarded her shrewdly, and Emma was glad that she could hold her own when it came to discussing quilt restoration and preservation. They had won a prestigious national award for their work, after all.

"Since this is such a valuable and historic piece, we've decided to do conservation rather than restoration." Emma pointed, careful not to touch the damaged areas. "In areas where the fabric is frayed, we'll add structural support underneath and add a fine mesh layer on top. You won't be able to see what we've done unless you use a magnifying glass. Our work will prevent further deterioration."

Sam nodded in approval. "You have the necessary experience to undertake this task?"

Kelly jumped in. "We certainly do." She listed the training she and Emma had taken and some of the projects they'd worked on. "In a couple of weeks, we're being recognized by the National Preservation Alliance for our work on a Civil War potholder quilt."

He snapped his fingers. "I read about that quilt in the Massachusetts Heritage Society newsletter. Another rare quilt. Bravo." He smiled at Priscilla. "Quite a coup to get these two."

Priscilla looked pleased. "I hire only the best."

That was a stretch, as Bart had commissioned the job, but Emma let it slide. The appraiser's endorsement might give them continued access to the Tolliver mansion, and that was what counted. "Thank you, Miss Tolliver. Considering the quilt's age and condition, it would be a good idea to leave it here rather than take it to our shop. We'll just need to set up a frame and a work table."

Priscilla tugged on one of the bedposts. "Maybe we can move this bed out. Bring your equipment in."

No! Emma thought quickly. The shirt would be discovered if the bed was moved. "That sounds fine. We'll get our equipment and arrange with Nate to help us take down the bed and set up our work area. You don't have to worry about it."

"When can you start?" Priscilla didn't seem concerned about finding out their fee before proceeding. Apparently the appraiser's approval had convinced her their work would be worth the cost, whatever that was.

"We'll need to finish our estimate and scope of work," Kelly said. "Then we'll know what materials we need. So, a couple of days, probably."

Sam, not interested in the turn the conversation had

taken, had doffed his gloves and was wandering around the room studying gilt-framed oil paintings of landscapes and flowers, making notes about each one on his tablet. "Very nice. Very nice indeed." He turned to Priscilla. "Tell me, dear lady," he said, injecting a roguish tone into his voice, "are the rumors true?"

Priscilla cocked her head and smiled slyly. "That depends which rumors you're referring to."

Emma exchanged a glance with Kelly. Was Sam talking about the treasure?

"I'm speaking of concealed doorways and hidden staircases." He lowered his voice into a confidential growl. "I'm partial to secret passageways. Always have been, ever since I read my first Hardy Boys book."

"Actually, we do have one," Priscilla said. "Would you like to see it?"

Sam gave a mock shudder of fear. "Are there ghosts?" He shuddered again. "I rather hope there are. Such fun."

"Those rumors are false," Priscilla said with a quelling glare. "No ghosts here. They wouldn't dare."

"I love secret doorways too," Kelly said, her eyes lighting up. "Can we come along?"

"I don't see why not, but I hate to interrupt your work."

Emma refrained from commenting that they had already been interrupted. "We just have a little more to do. Give us half an hour?" She bit her lip, hoping they would be allowed to see the passageway. In addition to being interesting, it might relate to Bart's death somehow. Regarding the quilt, she and Kelly could dispense with their usual examination and estimation process. Priscilla already had told them they had the job, so they could just bill for actual costs.

Priscilla looked at Sam for his input. "That works for me,"

he said. "I haven't had a chance to poke around the rest of the bedrooms yet."

They arranged to swing back by. Before continuing their work, Emma insisted on washing her hands in the adjacent bathroom. She lathered up twice, hoping to cleanse away the shock of touching stiff dried blood on an otherwise soft garment.

"Let's swap over," Emma said when she came back into the room. "I'll take notes." She stood at the bureau and Kelly picked up the magnifying glass and bent over the quilt. "We've done the top half."

"There's quite a bit of fraying at the bottom," Kelly said. "The silk they used is falling apart." She called out information to Emma about the blocks where damage was found. "I'm glad we're conserving. It'd be a bear matching all these old fabrics. Some of the pieces are tiny. So intricate."

After the visual examination, they took a series of photographs with a digital camera. They would enlarge the photographs on the store computer to study the quilt further and finalize the conservation methods and a plan of attack. The final step was writing up an estimate with the deposit amount stated.

Priscilla and Sam came back just as Emma and Kelly finished packing up. Feeling a little like Nancy Drew, Emma tucked the magnifying glass into her jeans pocket. She was hoping they would find something that would exonerate Dottie Faye or, at the very least, cast enough doubt to clear her name. Identifying Bart's killer would be a bonus.

Priscilla led them down the hall to the rear bedroom opposite Bart's office. Like the office and the other rooms at each end of the house, it boasted an enormous fireplace. "We have four outside chimneys on this house," she said, "a noted characteristic of the Federal style."

Emma remembered Nate saying that the line of chimneys marked the tunnel routes through town, since the wide chimney bases helped support entrances to the underground structures.

"The chimneys are obvious, but the stairs hidden in the stacks are not." She went to the paneling beside the fireplace and moved a piece of molding. As they watched, a hidden narrow door swung open into the room.

Sam cried out in amazement, clapping his hands. "How perfect. I wonder how many secret trysts have been facilitated by this little staircase."

Priscilla cast him a reproving look. "There were better uses for the stairs than illicit love affairs, I assure you." She reached into her pocket and pulled out three penlights and passed them out. "It's dark in there, so shine these at your feet as we go down the stairs." She picked up a bigger flashlight from the mantle.

The older woman squeezed through the opening, and the others followed. Emma turned on her penlight as they entered a small chamber that appeared to extend behind the fireplace. Priscilla shined her light around the area, which was empty and just large enough to hold the four of them standing. "This was used to hide runaway slaves. Not a bad little spot since the fireplace kept it warm."

Emma's light examined the wooden ceiling formed by the floor of the attic and the brick walls of the enclosure. It was surprisingly free from dust and cobwebs, fortunately. She imagined what it must have been like for fugitives enclosed here, hoping this house was the last stop on their way to freedom in Canada.

Sam shifted an ill-fitting brick in the back of the

fireplace, at about eye height. "Ooh. A hidey-hole. For treasure, perhaps?"

Priscilla shined the light into the empty crevice. "No, just another loose brick. This place needs constant maintenance." She moved toward the far corner. "The stairs are this way."

"So, the rumors of Benjamin Tolliver's treasure are false?" Sam asked. His little light bobbing, he followed Priscilla into inky darkness, onto the set of triangular steps twisting their way down.

"I'm afraid so. Watch your step."

"Liar," Kelly whispered.

Emma paused at the opening. She wasn't fond of tight, dark spaces.

"I'll go first," Kelly said. "Unless you want me behind you."

"No. Go first. That way I'll have your light too."

Kelly entered the staircase, placing her foot carefully on the narrow step. "Thank goodness for flashlights. Imagine using a candle and having it go out."

"No thanks." Emma took a deep breath and followed. She took the first cautious step down, pausing to shine the light on the next step to keep from stumbling. The way the steps circled reminded her of a spiral staircase. Probably built that way to save space. At least it was better than a ladder. Emma hated ladders.

Like the hidden chamber, the stairs were surprisingly clean, which indicated they had been used recently. *Did Priscilla include this route on her tours?* She'd have to ask. Or maybe it had been used for a more sinister purpose. Emma slowed even further and carefully examined each tread by the pinpoint beam of the flashlight.

She spotted a blotch even darker than the aged wood,

right in the corner where the step met the wall. Resting one hand on the wall and bracing her feet, she hunkered down and peered at it closely.

Was it a stain made by spilled food or drink as servants carried provisions to the hidden room? Or was it something more recent?

thirteen

"Emma? Are you all right?" Kelly called up the staircase.

"Oh ... I just stopped to tie my shoe." Emma gave that excuse in case her voice carried to Priscilla or Sam below.

Kelly's flashlight bounced off the walls as she climbed back up. "You can't fool me," she said softly. "What did you find?"

Emma placed the flashlight on the step so she could dig the magnifying glass out of her pocket. She shined the light onto the magnified spot, feeling like Encyclopedia Brown, another favorite fictional detective. "I'm not sure. It's a dark brown stain."

Kelly crouched down, and Emma handed her the magnifier. "It might be blood."

"It's hard to know without tests. And it could be ancient." Emma's excitement faded. She was probably grasping at straws. But they still had the shirt, and she knew that was significant.

Kelly wasn't so easily discouraged. "Maybe the murderer came down this way." She looked back up the staircase and counted. "I don't want to mark it in case the wrong person sees that." Pulling out her phone, she took a picture of the stain, using the flash. "Maybe if we blow it up, we can see more detail."

"You're right, Kelly."

The faint murmur of Priscilla and Sam's voices drifted up the staircase. "We'd better go," Emma said.

They hurried down the rest of the way—Emma resolutely ignoring her discomfort—and emerged into the kitchen right beside the massive fireplace.

"That was really interesting. Thanks, Miss Tolliver," Kelly said, beaming.

"It was indeed," Sam said. He glanced at his watch. "I'd better be going, but I'll call to schedule a meeting later this week with you and the team, Priscilla. Then we can get started on a full-scale appraisal. How's that?" The appraiser had moved up in rank to a first-name basis, Emma noticed.

"That sounds fine. I'll show you out." She turned to Emma and Kelly. "If you've got an estimate ready, I'll write you a check for the deposit."

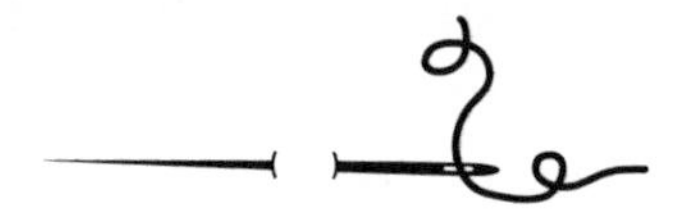

The Lantern Cove Bank and Trust was situated on the town square, presently the center of Pirate Days revelry. Emma finally found a parking spot down by a waterfront warehouse behind the Crow's Nest Café.

"Let's have lunch after we go to the bank," Kelly said, putting a hand on her midriff. "I'm starving."

The delectable smell of French fries and hamburgers drifted from the restaurant. Emma's stomach gurgled in response. "Let's. And maybe we can get Olivia's DNA while we're at it."

"That's my girl." Kelly winked. "Always on the job."

They crossed the street and worked their way around the edge of the village green. In keeping with the pirate theme, booths offered knot-tying lessons, themed crafts and trinkets, and photo opportunities with seafaring rogues. A treasure hunt for children had them scurrying around the green looking for clues. In addition, the event offered a game arcade, rides, and an assortment of food found at such fairs.

Kelly groaned as they passed a sausage booth. "I don't know if I can make it back to the café."

"Sure you can." Emma paused to buy her a bag of caramel popcorn with peanuts. "This will tide you over."

"*Tide*, huh? No pun intended, right?" Kelly grabbed the bag and began munching. "I feel kind of out of place. Most people are wearing costumes. Or at least a hat or eye patch."

She was right. Even the employees inside the small bank—a haven of cool dignity compared to the festivities beyond its doors—were in period garb.

"I'm starting to think this town is a little obsessed with costumes," Kelly whispered to Emma as they approached the line for the tellers who were dressed as wenches. "Remember Priscilla's old-fashioned costume the day we met her?"

Emma did remember and it reminded her of something she'd heard that day, something Priscilla had said. But before she had a chance to tell Kelly, it was their turn in line and they were called to one of the windows.

"We're here to claim back part of our treasure," Kelly said, smiling at the young woman waiting on them as she handed her Priscilla's check, drawn on her personal account.

It took her a second to understand what Kelly meant with her reference to pirate loot. The teller laughed and peered at the check. "Do you have an account here?"

"No," Emma said. "We'd like to cash it." Later they would deposit the money in their own account in Mystic Harbor. Otherwise they might have to wait a couple of days for the check to clear. In view of this plan, they had asked Priscilla to make the check out to Emma Cotton and Kelly Grace instead of Cotton & Grace.

"I'll need to see IDs," the teller said, as expected.

Emma and Kelly dug their licenses out of their wallets.

"People seem to enjoy wearing costumes in Lantern Cove," Emma said casually as she slid her license across the marble counter. "When we met Priscilla Tolliver, she was wearing period dress from the 1800s. And Pirate Days hadn't even started yet."

Kelly caught on. "She was wearing a giant bonnet." She giggled, gesturing around her head to indicate the shape of the big hat. "I've never seen such a thing outside television and the movies."

The teller laughed as she peered at the licenses. "That's because of the museum her brother started." Her mouth turned down in a frown, and she lowered her voice to a hush, glancing both ways to make sure no one was listening. "He was such a nice man. Priscilla was here that day, apparently while he was being killed. She told me what a shock it was to return from errands and find his body."

"That does sound dreadful." Emma made her eyes big, as though enthralled by the teller's tale. "So, you saw her just before?"

The teller shook her head. "Not in person. She came through the drive-through. I remember that. That's what she does most days. It's more convenient than finding a place to park." She pushed buttons on the computer keyboard and processed the check then counted out bills and tucked them into a small envelope. Smiling, she slid it toward Emma. "Have a nice day."

"I'd forgotten Priscilla mentioning going to the bank that morning," Kelly said once they were back outside, walking through the raucous festival toward the café.

Emma dropped coins into a bucket set near a pirate with a wooden leg playing sea shanties on the accordion. He gave her a gap-toothed grin of appreciation. "I've been thinking a lot about alibis and who has them. I guess we can cross Priscilla off the list of suspects."

"And it looks like Nate has moved to the top of the list. The bloody shirt is similar to the ones we've seen him wearing." They reached Water Street and were lucky enough to get the walk signal at the corner.

"We need to find out more about his alibi. Maybe the killer is someone we don't know about, and he knew the other two were going to be out of the house."

"Or he got lucky." Kelly pushed open the café door.

Inside, the place was half full. Sarah, the waitress who had served them before, seated them at a booth in the back with a view of the waterfront. "I guess a lot of people are eating at the fair," Kelly said as she studied the menu.

Sarah brought them water then pulled out her pad. "What can I get you?"

"I'm having the seafood chowder," Emma said. "Yes, it's hot out, but I can't resist fresh-caught scallops, shrimp, clams, and haddock. And iced tea to drink, please."

"Good choice," Kelly said. "I'll have the same. And a basket of your homemade rolls with butter, please."

"They're coming out of the oven as we speak," Sarah said.

She quickly returned with deep bowls of piping hot soup and the promised rolls.

"This is heaven," Kelly said, buttering a hot roll.

"I agree. We've been all over the world on our case, and some of the best food we've had is right here in Massachusetts." Emma swallowed a savory spoonful of the rich broth dotted with morsels of tender seafood.

"I guess we're real Yankees."

"Don't tell Dottie Faye that." Emma giggled and Kelly joined in.

"What did I tell you about being late?"

Emma looked up to see Olivia in the hallway leading to

the restrooms, facing away from the tables in the restaurant. Whoever she was talking to stood in the shadows beyond.

"Who's she talking to?" Kelly whispered. Her back was to Olivia.

"I can't tell ... oh, it's Mandy. You know, the other waitress."

"You missed the lunch rush, and I had to wait tables for you," Olivia said, hands on hips. Her high-piled red hair shook as she nodded her head in emphasis. "That's not acceptable."

"Why? You're too good to wait tables?" Mandy's lip curled in a sneer.

"That's not the point. I hired you for a job, and I expect you to do it."

"Or what?" Mandy gave Olivia an insolent glare. Arms crossed in front of her chest, she tapped her foot. "You'll fire me?" She smirked. "You can't do that. Josh will walk if you fire me. And you need him."

"He's a good cook, sure. But he can be replaced. Now, are you taking your section or leaving? Your choice."

Mandy flounced past Olivia and out of the hallway. Emma quickly ducked her head, pretending to be intent on the contents of her bowl. Olivia entered the room and seeing Emma and Kelly, veered over toward them with a wan smile of greeting. Kelly slid over and let her sit.

"How are you today, Olivia?" Emma asked.

Olivia sighed, propping her chin on one hand. "Working for yourself isn't all it's cracked up to be some days."

"We're self-employed too and wouldn't trade it for anything," Kelly said. "Of course, a quilting shop is a little less stressful than a restaurant."

"Do you have employees?" At their headshake, she said. "Enough said."

To lighten the tone, Emma said, "Well, not official ones. But my aunt and Kelly's mother often work for us."

Olivia shuddered. "Relatives? God bless you."

"Speaking of which ..." Kelly pulled out her phone. "I'll just text Mom and tell her we'll be back soon."

"Good idea." Emma pulled the basket closer and fished for another roll. "Can we buy you a cup of coffee or tea?" This time they would take her cup if they had to wrest it from the waitress's hand.

"No thanks. How is the chowder?" Olivia nodded toward Emma's bowl.

Emma squelched her disappointment. *Move on to plan B, whatever that is.* They had to get her DNA soon. "Fantastic, like everything you serve." She broke the roll in half and buttered it.

The front door jangled and Nate entered. Noticing them sitting together, he headed over without waiting to be seated. Emma slid over so he could sit in the booth. He, too, peered at their bowls. "I'll have that."

Olivia waved Sarah over, and she took Nate's order. Again, Emma offered to buy Olivia something to drink, but she said no. Mandy appeared to have settled down into her task, and they heard her pealing laughter at a table by the window where two men were seated.

"I wish she'd be that agreeable with me," Olivia said.

"What do you mean?" Nate asked. He picked up a straw, took off the paper, and stuck it into his iced tea.

"Oh, she's a good waitress. When she wants to be. But she's always late, and she's quite mouthy." She gave her brother a rueful smile. "Now I know why you broke up with her."

He ducked his head and squeezed his lemon into his tea. "That's not quite what happened, but OK."

Emma's ears perked up. Nate and the tempestuous Mandy were once boyfriend and girlfriend?

"She keeps threatening me whenever I try to confront her or set rules," Olivia said. "She says she'll walk out and if she does, Josh will too."

"Would he really leave his job if she did?" Kelly asked.

"I don't know. I don't want to put it to the test. He's got a loyal following, and if there's one thing you don't want to mess with in a restaurant, it's the food. He goes and his recipes go too."

"He's been here a long time, then," Emma said.

"He used to own this place. But he wasn't as good at managing as at cooking. He basically ran the place into the ground. Buying it was ideal, really. Many times you buy a restaurant, you have to start over building a clientele. This place isn't hugely profitable, but it was breaking even from day one." She paused as Sarah brought Nate's soup and refilled their iced tea from a pitcher.

"Watch what happens now that Priscilla's involved," Nate said after Sarah left. "She has a habit of messing things up." He went on to tell his sister the arrangement he'd come to with the heir to the mansion. "I've got another few weeks, and then I'm out."

"So she's going to sell everything, huh?" Olivia shook her head, her lips compressed. "I guess she doesn't care at all about what her brother wanted."

"I'd say not. She had an appraiser there today and the will hasn't even been probated yet."

"It's too bad you didn't find the treasure," Olivia said, her eyes dreamy. "That would solve a lot of problems." She turned to Emma and Kelly. "Have you heard about the fabled Tolliver treasure?"

"Oh, yes," Kelly said. "We've seen the tunnel map."

"It's too bad the clue to where it is exactly hasn't surfaced," Emma said innocently, to see how Nate and Olivia would react.

"I'm going to keep looking," Nate said, hunched over his chowder. He took a big slurping spoonful and swallowed. "But even if I find the treasure, it won't help us financially. Bart was going to leave it to charity, according to his will. I just want to find it for my thesis. And as a contribution to my field, of course—early American history."

Emma was struck with a thought, and judging by Kelly's raised eyebrows, she had the same realization. What did Bart's will say? They needed to find out.

fourteen

Outside the café, Kelly looked up probate court information on her phone. "The courthouse in Salem handles Lantern Cove wills." She pushed a few more icons. "And they're open. Let's go."

"You're sure they'll let us look at Bart's will?" Emma asked as they walked down the sidewalk.

"Absolutely." Kelly wove around a family with twins in a stroller. "When Dad died, I helped Mom with the estate paperwork. Our attorney filed his will at the probate court, and it was open to public view."

"I guess you learn something new every day." Emma almost stepped on Kelly's heels as she stopped short right in front of her in the thick crowd of fairgoers.

"I can't believe it." Kelly pointed to a booth with a sign reading: Original Fried Jellybeans. I had those at the Big E." The Big E was the nickname for the Eastern States Exposition held in western Massachusetts every year.

"I can't believe it, either," Emma said. "You ate fried jellybeans?"

"I sure did." Kelly started walking again, glancing back at the booth longingly. "And now I have a craving."

"Go ahead, buy some. I'll wait." Emma shook her head, smiling at her friend's voracious and varied appetite. "At least they're a little better for you than fried butter. I heard about that on television."

"I've had that too. They can—and do—fry just about

anything." Kelly scurried to the booth and got in line. Within minutes, she had her tasty treat. "See? They're not so bad."

Emma peered at the fried jellybeans, which looked like lumps of fried dough studded with melted candies. "Maybe I'll try a bite."

"Yellow, red, green, or blue?"

"Not blue. I hate eating anything blue except blueberries." Emma took a red-stained morsel and popped it into her mouth, chewing as she dug out the Jeep keys. Not terrible, but the best she could say about it was that she had tried fried jellybeans. Eric's daughter, Riley, would get a kick out of that, and she filed the experience away to tell her when they went on the whale watch later in the month. Thinking of Riley—and Eric— reminded her of his offer to help plan the award event. The date was approaching fast.

"We haven't done a stitch of planning for the award event yet," Emma said as they drove out of Lantern Cove toward Salem. "And it's next week. Maybe we can talk about it at Nimble Thimbles tomorrow."

"That sounds like a plan. We've been too busy at the store and with our cases to even think about it." Kelly groaned. "And I thought staying home for a change while investigating Olivia would give us more spare time. Fat chance." Their prior investigations of suspects had taken them to far-flung places, including New York City, Arizona, Ireland, and England. While Kelly enjoyed travel, she fretted over being away from her husband and college-aged children too long.

"It will be over soon, I hope. Then we can go back to ordinary life permanently." As she drove, Emma took in the lush country landscape bordering the coastal road, allowing its peaceful beauty to give her respite. Summer was her favorite season, enjoyed for its warm temperatures, flowers, birds, and good times with family and friends.

"I can't believe we didn't get Olivia's DNA today," Kelly said. "If we don't get it soon, I'm going to tackle her and take it by force." She laughed to show she was joking. "The assault charge might be worth it."

"Yes, it is frustrating. I hate to tip our hand and ask, although we've done it before." Then she thought of something. "Do you think Nate's DNA would work? Since they're siblings?"

"Maybe. Let's ask the lab if his would be sufficient. That can be our plan B."

Emma slowed as they approached the outskirts of Salem. "Give me directions from here, will you?"

Like Mystic Harbor and Lantern Cove, Salem was a quaint city founded in Colonial times. Salem made the most of its somewhat checkered history of witch trials by offering a witch museum, tours of historic houses, and spooky attractions, although Emma preferred the architecture, literature, and art associated with the town.

One fine historic example was the probate court, a massive stone structure with Ionic columns built in 1909. After wandering the hushed, cool hallways, they found the clerk's office and requested Bart's will. After a short wait, the clerk brought the file to the counter for them to read.

"The Last Will and Testament of Bartholomew Benjamin Tolliver" wasn't long, and it wasn't complicated. Everything had been left to his sister, Priscilla, as might be expected. If she predeceased him, it all went to charity. The most interesting provision was related to Benjamin Tolliver's treasure, described as an emerald-and-diamond necklace, gold coins, and associated items. Should it be located after his death, Nathaniel Dexter Stewart was to receive half the proceeds of its value. The other half was to go to the Lantern Cove Historical Society.

They paid for a copy of the will and exited the room into the hall, away from listening ears. "The treasure provision is another interesting twist regarding motive," Emma said. "Yes, Nate is entitled to half of it. But if Bart had still been alive when it was found, wouldn't he have done the same thing—shared it?"

"It really is a puzzle," Kelly agreed. "Priscilla has an alibi, but the best motive. Bart's estate must be worth millions."

"I wonder how much of it belongs to the nonprofit. Do you think Patrick could help us look into that?"

Kelly held the front door of the courthouse open for Emma. "I'm sure he'd love to. His dream career is to be a forensic accountant and help track down the bad guys."

"Great. We can use him on our team."

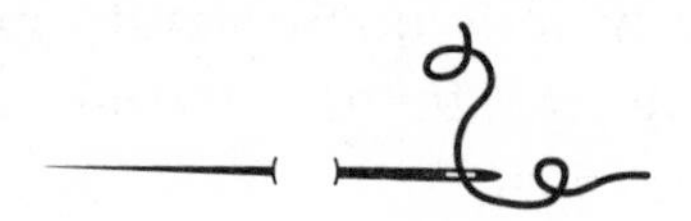

"Thanks for getting these, Emma," Marcia Goode said, taking two pints of locally grown blueberries out of Emma's hands. "Do they need to be washed?"

"No, I rinsed them myself." Emma glanced at the buffet table in the Nimble Thimbles meeting room above Uncommon Threads. Marcia had created a colorful and attractive fruit, yogurt, and granola breakfast rounded out with muffins and croissants from Grounds for Suspicion. Hot coffee and tea were also available.

Marcia tipped the blueberries into a yellow pottery bowl

and added a spoon. "Help yourselves, everyone," she called to the other members.

Another full house, Emma noted, greeting everyone as they lined up to eat. After getting a cup of coffee and a bowl of vanilla yogurt topped with strawberries, pineapple, and blueberries, she found a seat between Dottie Faye and Kelly.

"Did you have a good night?" Kelly asked.

"It was fine," Emma lied. Instead of being tired after another busy day running around, she'd been too keyed up to sleep. First she stayed up way later than her usual bedtime reading a book, Ichabod curled next to her on the bed, and then she lay awake with the two cases churning in her head.

"I didn't sleep a wink," Kelly said. "And you know that's not like me."

Emma stared at her friend. "I didn't either." They both burst into laughter.

"How's everything going with the Rose investigation?" Walter asked.

"Any news in the Bart Tolliver murder?" Tokala's dark eyes were concerned as they rested on Dottie Faye.

Emma held up a hand. "We have new information on both, but first, everyone, let's talk about our award ceremony. It keeps getting pushed off due to everything else we've been worried about."

"Yeah, I'm worried about digesting my breakfast," Kelly joked, rubbing her midriff. The group hooted and laughed. Kelly's ironclad stomach and hearty appetite were well-known.

"That's what happens as you get older," Dottie Faye said sagely. "The digestion is the first to go."

"Gosh, I sure hope not." Kelly looked horrified. "I'll have to find a new hobby."

Marcia got up and poured herself another cup of coffee. "There are three things to decide. Guest list, agenda, and food. Let's start with the agenda."

"I want to keep it low-key and casual," Emma said. "Fun."

"Me too." Kelly nodded in agreement. "So, we could have opening remarks—for about a minute—then the award can be presented. The preservation people might want to say something. Then Emma and I can say thank you. And that's it."

"I'll handle the opening remarks," Marcia said, "since I nominated you."

"That'd be great, Marcia," Emma said.

"If you invite the mayor, she'll want to speak," Walter said.

"True," Maeve said. "We'll give her a minute, and then I'll pull her off stage with my hook." Everyone laughed. The mayor of Mystic Harbor was notoriously long-winded.

"That sounds like enough speakers," Kelly said. "We don't want to bore people."

"That's settled, then," Dottie Faye said. "What about the guest list? I think we should plan for one hundred."

"That many people? Surely not." Emma couldn't imagine who beyond family and friends would want to come to the event.

"Let's count everyone up," Marcia said.

Holly Locke took notes as people called out the number in their family and named the people who absolutely should be there.

"Don't forget the press," Marcia said. "And the city council will need invites."

To Emma's surprise, the total did indeed rise to nearly one hundred. "Where are we going to fit all those people? Do you think we should have it somewhere besides Cotton & Grace?"

"I don't," Kelly said. "It's a great chance to promote the store. We'll figure it out."

"It'll work with some rearranging," Walter said. "You could move out the work tables and any items that aren't for sale."

"That's what we'll do," Kelly said, pulling out a notepad and taking notes. "Hopefully it'll be a nice day and we can leave the door open for people to stand on the sidewalk."

"What about food?" Maeve said. "We really don't want a lot of people eating and drinking inside the store. Something is sure to get spilled on the inventory."

"How about putting the refreshments outside?" Tokala suggested. "You could set up an awning in case it's raining."

"Great idea," Kelly said. "And why don't we ask the Chocolate Cauldron to cater? Then people could hang out on their sidewalk as well. That'll give us more room."

"You'll probably need a permit," Walter said. "I'll check with the city for you."

"Thanks, Walter," Emma said. "We'd better get right on that."

"I'll do it first thing Monday."

Kelly rubbed her hands together. "So, what should we have to eat?"

"I vote for tiny sandwiches, lemonade, and a big chocolate cake congratulating Emma and Kelly," Dottie Faye said. "Maybe mini cream puffs too."

"Yum," Holly said. "The Cauldron makes the best cake. Maybe they could illustrate it with a picture of the quilt you're getting the award for."

"That's a great idea," Tokala said.

"I'll take care of setting up the food and drinks on the day," Maeve said.

"Thanks so much, everyone," Emma said with a sigh. "I feel like this event is going to be a big success, thanks to you."

"Yes. Thanks, guys." Kelly gave Emma an innocent smile. "Don't forget to put Eric on the work list. He said he'd help."

"I won't," Emma said simply, not wanting to rise to the bait in front of the Nimble Thimbles. It was bad enough getting teased about her fledgling love life by Dottie Faye and Kelly.

"You'll need a few strong men to move things around," Walter said, flexing his arm. "And move them back, after. Everyone forgets that part."

"Patrick and Keith will help," Kelly said.

Marcia looked around at everyone's empty dishes. "If you're all done, let's clean up and get to work on the town history quilt."

"Anything new with the Rose Peterson case?" Walter asked again as they all began to stitch.

Emma explained that they hadn't been able to get Olivia's DNA yet but that Alex had a lead on Danielle finally.

"You're running out of suspects," Tokala pointed out. "I hope one of those women is the guilty party."

"Me too." Emma's heart sank at the possibility they would reach a dead end in the investigation. She prayed desperately that that wouldn't happen.

"I had a thought that there might be other suspects outside the students in Rose's class," Dottie Faye said, "so I got a DNA sample from the college president."

The group gasped at this announcement.

"How on earth did you manage that?" Marcia said.

With a smirk, Dottie Faye went on to tell the tale of her visit to President Coleman and her deft method of collecting his DNA. "Unfortunately," she concluded, "the results came back negative."

Everyone groaned in dismay. Then Walter laughed. "It doesn't say much for his reputation that we're all disappointed he's not a killer."

"What pretext did you use to get in?" Tokala asked. "He's notoriously stingy with his time, especially with the public."

Dottie Faye ducked her head and actually blushed. She hadn't mentioned the Rose Peterson scholarship, and Emma realized her aunt, usually so open about herself, didn't want it publicly known. She waved her hand and said vaguely, "I invited him to Emma and Kelly's award ceremony. He, of course, had the idea I might give the college money." She made it sound like a remote possibility.

"Good for you," Marcia said. "You're so resourceful. All of you are." She paused to thread her needle. "What's happening with the Bart Tolliver murder?" She leveled a compassionate look at Dottie Faye. "I speak for all of us when I say that you have our unqualified support." The group chimed in, murmuring agreement, and Maeve reached over and squeezed Dottie Faye's hand.

Dottie Faye lifted her chin. "My attorney is confident that they'll have to drop the charges. The medical examiner's report came in, and there's more evidence that I'm innocent." She snorted. "Which is to be expected, of course."

Emma hadn't heard the results of the medical examiner's report. "Tell us, Dottie Faye, what did it say?"

"I just found out this morning." Dottie Faye's smile was smug. "The report said that the killer was left-handed. The ME could tell by the angle of the wound." Dottie Faye waved her hands, her long nails painted a brilliant coral. "Anyone who knows me knows that my left hand is just useless. I can't even paint my own nails. I'm not ambi … whatever that word is."

"Ambidextrous." Emma's heart thumped. Nate Stewart was left-handed. He'd worn a brace, claiming to have an injury. *Was the injury faked to throw people off the scent? Had he hurt himself stabbing Bart?* Either was a possibility. She'd have to ask Eric for a doctor's opinion about the severity of his supposed condition.

As though reading her thoughts, Kelly told them about the shirt they found resembling the ones Nate wore and the fact that he benefited from Bart's will.

"He's entitled to a share of the treasure?" Walter said. "That sounds like a motive."

"Unless Bart was going to give it to him anyway," Emma pointed out. "Priscilla inherits everything but the treasure, according to the will."

"I asked Patrick about how Bart's nonprofit was set up," Kelly said. "And he told me that Bart apparently loaned—not gave—items to the museum, according to the report filed with the government. It has no assets except the bank account."

"That means that the collection is part of his estate," Dottie Faye said.

"Big motive for Priscilla, then," Walter said.

"But she has an alibi," Emma said. She shared what she and Kelly learned at the bank.

"I wonder if Nate has one," Tokala said. "Maybe you can find out while he's helping you locate that treasure."

"Ooh, are you still looking for the treasure! I hope you find it," Holly exclaimed. "We've been studying the salvage of pirate ships in history class, and it's amazing. They send submarines to explore sunken ships and the ocean floor."

"I'm glad we don't have to do that," Emma said wryly. "Going underground in a tunnel is scary enough for me."

"From what I know of Nate, he really seemed to care for

Bart," Dottie Faye said. "I find it hard to believe he killed him." She frowned, shaking her head. "I just can't picture it. He seems so mild-mannered, almost sweet."

"So do most serial killers," Kelly said wryly.

"That blood-stained shirt does seem incriminating," Marcia said. "But it really isn't conclusive. Didn't you say Nate lives there? Then anyone with access to the house could have worn it to kill Bart."

fifteen

"It looks like it's going to be a busy Saturday, judging by the number of people downtown this morning." Kelly unlocked the front door of Cotton & Grace, and Emma and Dottie Faye followed her inside, Emma pausing to flick on the light switches.

Kelly went to the cash register to log on and Dottie Faye disappeared into the back room.

"What's she up to?" Emma asked. She checked over the window display, tweaking bags and baby quilts and accessories into a more attractive arrangement. They'd adorned the display area with potted plants and they needed watering. Maybe Dottie Faye was filling the watering can.

"I have no idea," Kelly said. Finished counting the loose bills and coins, she shut the drawer. "Do you mind if I go on a coffee run next door? I can pick up their catering menu at the same time." Crouching down, she turned on the music, selecting light classical befitting a breezy summer day.

"That'd be fine." The door chime sounded and Emma turned to see a party of four women entering the shop, voices raised in excitement at seeing the inventory. "But be quick. It looks like your prediction was right." Smiling, she hurried to the counter. "Let me know if you need help, ladies."

"What can I do?" Dottie Faye asked, smoothing her shell pink linen suit as she emerged from the back room, a furtive yet smug expression on her face.

Emma noticed she was empty-handed. "How about

watering the plants? Then you can take the register while I help people."

Kelly soon returned with coffee and pastries, just in time to assist another group of customers thronging into the shop. In addition to buying ready-made items, several wanted to consult with Emma and Kelly about quilt repair and restoration. Emma scheduled several people for appointments the following week. It wasn't until an hour later that Emma realized what Dottie Faye must have been doing.

Dr. Eric Hart entered the shop, looking around in trepidation at the chattering groups of women filling the place. Spotting Emma, relief slid over his face. With nods and smiles of greeting, he wound his way through the crowd to the design desk where Emma sat loading photographs of the Tolliver quilt into the computer.

"Good morning, Eric," she said. "What brings you here?" She finished uploading the files and removed the digital card from the computer then tucked it back into the digital camera.

"I heard you needed help, and I had some free time." White teeth flashed against his tan as he grinned down at her.

"Dottie Faye called you, right?" At his nod, she glanced toward Dottie Faye, who was working the cash register. She could tell by the twitchiness of her shoulders and the resolute refusal to look over that Dottie Faye knew full well that Emma was on to her.

Well, Eric was here, so she might as well put him to work. "I do need your help, actually. We're going to have to move a lot of stuff out of this room for the award ceremony in a few days." Moving the racks of inventory and the worktables and desks was going to be a lot of work. Emma sighed. "Not today, of course, but I could use some help devising a plan. What stays, what goes, see if we can cram everything into the back room." She explained to him the basic agenda they'd decided upon and that as many as one hundred people might attend.

Eric whistled. "Wow. That would be fantastic. I can see what you mean about rearranging everything. You need to clear a space for people to stand. Maybe push the inventory for sale against the walls and store whatever isn't for sale. You want them to be able to spend money while they're here. Kill two birds and all that."

Emma stared at Eric in admiration, appreciating his quick grasp of the situation. "That's exactly right. We can display the award-winning quilt against the back wall so everyone can see it. The presenters can stand in front of it."

Eric followed her to the back room where boxes of inventory and materials were stored. "If we rearrange those boxes, we'll be able to put more on the shelves. And I think I can get the tables in here. They fold, right? And one of the desks."

"Actually, we need to take one of the tables over to the Tolliver mansion for a quilt job. We could use the other upstairs for our design projects. Get it out of the way but still allow us to keep using it." Emma led Eric up the narrow stairs to the cozy studio apartment.

"I didn't even know this was up here. It's cute." He walked around the main room and into the kitchenette. "You're right. A worktable will fit along the wall under the window. One of those desks would be hard to get up the stairs. It's pretty narrow."

"Emma?" Kelly's voice called. "Are you up there?"

"I'll be right down," Emma called back. To Eric, she said, "Let's do that today, if you have time."

"I sure do." He pulled at his navy polo shirt. "That's why I wore this old shirt and jeans."

"No golf?" Emma gave him a teasing smile.

"Later. Three o'clock tee time for nine holes." Eric smiled back, and as their eyes met, Emma felt a shift in the air between them, a blossoming sense of warm intimacy and understanding. For a few moments, seconds really, she allowed herself to bask in the glow. Then she blinked and broke the spell, suddenly all too aware that they were alone in a private space for the first time. His clinical, antiseptic-smelling doctor's office didn't count. Wrenching her eyes away, she turned and headed for the stairs, uneasy and confused by her own feelings.

"They have a great brunch at the country club," he said. "I know it's short notice, but will you go with me tomorrow after church?"

As she clattered down the stairs, an image of lunching at the elegant country club with Eric, sitting poolside perhaps, flashed into her mind. She wasn't ready for alone time with him, but she did enjoy dates—public dates. "Sure. Sounds like fun."

"Excellent. I'll make reservations."

Kelly stood at the foot of the stairs, watching them descend with amusement in her eyes. "A courier just delivered the potholder quilt." She gave Eric a cheeky grin. "Hi, Eric."

"Morning, Kelly. I'll go get that table, Emma."

As he disappeared into the shop, Kelly nudged Emma. "What was going on up there?"

Emma blushed. "Nothing. He's helping us rearrange the shop. I thought we could put the design jobs up in the apartment until after the award ceremony. Get them out of the way."

"Let's put the potholder quilt upstairs too, until we display it."

The valuable quilt had been delivered rolled in a long tube. After Eric took the table upstairs, Emma asked him to carry the quilt up and set it on the daybed. The next hour or so went like that, with Eric helping carry projects upstairs and rearranging the back room. He even went to a neighboring store to borrow a tall stepladder so he could replace a bulb in one of the antique hanging lights.

"Do we need this ladder for anything else before I take it back?" Eric asked as he lugged it over to the counter.

"I don't know about the ladder, but I think we need you to come around on a regular basis," Kelly said, half seriously. "You've been a lot of help."

"He sure has," Dottie Faye said, batting thick eyelashes as she looked Eric up and down. "It's wonderful having a man around the place."

Clasping the ladder with one arm, he stood a little taller, pleased at their appreciation.

"Why don't you lay it on a little thicker, Dottie Faye," Emma murmured. Louder, she added, "I think we're finished with the ladder, Eric. Thank Joe for me, won't you? And thank you for all your help."

"No problem. It's been a nice change. I've had fun hanging out with you ladies."

"I think we owe Eric lunch for all he's done," Kelly said. "Shall I do a sandwich run?" She quickly jotted down everyone's order and called it in to Grounds for Suspicion while Eric left to take back the ladder. "They added a delivery service," she called in triumph after disconnecting the call. "We never have to leave here again for provisions."

"That's handy," Emma said. "Speaking of provisions, let's look at the Cauldron menu and make our picks since business seems to be in a lull right this minute." Their customers apparently had been struck with hunger at the same time, and the store was temporarily deserted. By the time Eric returned from his errand, they'd decided on the assortment of sandwiches and pastries to order for the award event.

He entered the store through the back room, having used the alley to deliver the ladder to its owner. In his hand, he held one red rose.

Dottie Faye gasped, putting a hand to her chest. "Oh, my. A red rose. The sign of true love."

Emma stared at it, stunned. He really hadn't gone and bought a rose, had he? That seemed over-the-top considering the stage of their relationship. Had she sent the wrong signals? And what was he thinking, delivering it in front of everyone?

Eric flushed brick red under his tan. "I'm sorry. I didn't buy this. I found it at the back door, lying on the stoop. One of you must have a secret admirer."

Emma was embarrassed by her assumption. What a fool she was.

"We don't have an admirer." Kelly looked on in horror. "We have a stalker." She recited the "Blood is red" poem Emma had gotten.

"A stalker left this?" Eric waved the rose then tossed it on the counter. He dashed to the back door, followed by Kelly and eventually Emma, when she snapped out of her stupor. Bursting out the door, they gazed up and down the alley. No one was out there, except a white-aproned cook stealing a smoke outside a pub a few doors up.

Eric called to him. "Did you see someone leave something at this doorway?"

The cook shook his head. "No, man. I just got out here." He waved his barely burned cigarette for emphasis.

Back inside the shop, Eric got very serious. "Tell me about this guy."

The three of them filled him in on all the events they'd

suffered since beginning their investigation into Rose's death.

"We're planning to trap him," Emma said. "I'm tired of his harassment."

Eric narrowed his eyes in concern. "What kind of trap? That sounds dangerous."

"We're using the potholder quilt as bait," Kelly explained. "Tomorrow we're phoning invites to our two chief suspects for a special VIP event on Monday afternoon. Then we'll cancel it Monday morning. Knowing our prowler, he'll break in Sunday night and try to ruin it for us."

"Maybe." Eric's tone was skeptical. "What if those two aren't responsible?"

Emma shrugged. "Then we'll know that, right? We have to start somewhere."

Eric thought about it, tapping one foot as he rubbed his chin, elbow cupped in his hand. "I want to help," he finally said. "I don't want you facing a thug like that alone."

He paced about. "So, the quilt will be in that corner. Is your aim to get evidence of him breaking in or are you going to physically detain him?"

Emma and Kelly exchanged glances. "We can't let him actually touch the potholder quilt," Emma said. "It's priceless. So, we have to let him come in but stop him from harming the quilt."

"What if he's wearing a mask? Then video will be useless," Kelly said. "We have to find out who it is."

"I agree. Trap him and then call the police. They won't be able to ignore your problem after catching him breaking and entering." Eric grinned. "You shouldn't risk harm coming to that quilt, though. If he's like most men, er, people, he wouldn't know a potholder quilt if it bit him. So, how about putting up a decoy? Just for that night?"

"That's a great idea," Kelly said. "I have an old one that looks sort of like the potholder style."

The jingling of the door announced the arrival of customers, so Dottie Faye excused herself and went to wait on them.

"Do you have any ideas for a trap, Eric?" Emma asked. "I guess I haven't thought past the concept."

"I haven't either," Kelly said. "I keep thinking about a cage coming down from the ceiling like in the movies. Lights flashing and alarms going off."

Eric pointed to the ceiling. "How about a big fishing net? The ceiling is high enough that you won't spot it hanging up there in the dark. A trip wire can go off as he walks under the net and make it fall down on him. You need one of those old heavy ones with weights around the edges."

Kelly snapped her fingers. "I know where we can get one. At Bart's museum. Remember the pirate ship display? I saw some thick, heavy nets."

"That's right," Emma said. "Do you think we can borrow one?"

Kelly shrugged. "All we can do is ask."

"Why don't you two do that, and I'll give one of my buddies a call." Eric pulled out his cellphone. "He used to be in special ops, and he'll know how to set up a trip wire."

As he moved off toward the back room, Kelly pulled out her phone. "I got both the mansion and Priscilla's house number yesterday. I'll give her a call." She tried Priscilla's house first and got no answer. "I'll try the mansion. Maybe she's over there."

As she listened, she circled her hand around. "Ringing, ringing," she mouthed. Then her brows rose as someone finally picked up. "Is this Nate? Is Priscilla there? She's not?"

Emma could hear his voice over the phone, he was speaking so loudly. He explained that he didn't know where Priscilla was.

"We just called to see if we could borrow one of those old fishing nets you have in the museum for a couple of days. We need it for a display. We'll take good care of it."

Nate said that Priscilla wouldn't care since they weren't worth much. Then he went on so volubly that Emma couldn't catch what he was saying. If the shop hadn't been full of customers, she would have asked Kelly to put it on speaker.

"We'll come over later this afternoon. Don't touch anything until we get there, OK? See you then." She hung up.

"What was that all about?" Emma asked, her heart in her throat. "Did something else happen?" Ugly images rushed through her head. Had the killer struck again?

"No one's hurt. But Nate's pretty upset. Someone ransacked his room."

sixteen

Emma pictured the scene in Nate's ransacked room, bedding and clothing strewn everywhere. "Do you think they were looking for the shirt?"

Kelly tucked her phone in her pocket. "Either that or the map. Nate said the police came over and took a report, but they weren't much help, especially since he couldn't tell if anything was missing. When we go over later to pick up the net, let's take the work table so we can set up the room and tuck that shirt somewhere else."

"Great idea. Handling the quilt will give us an excuse to wear gloves." Emma shuddered. "I'm not going to get any more of my DNA on that thing. I shouldn't have touched it in the first place."

"If you hadn't, it might have disappeared."

Eric came back into the store. "I'm meeting with my friend later. He's going to help design a trip wire for the net. Did you find one?"

"Yes," Kelly said. "In Lantern Cove."

He glanced at the big store clock. "If you don't need me for anything else, I guess I'll head out for my golf match."

"There is just one more little thing," Emma said. Usually she and Kelly handled their own equipment for jobs, but Emma was enjoying having Eric around to help, she had to admit. "Can you help load a frame and that work table into my Jeep?" She pointed. "We're taking them over to Lantern Cove when we pick up the net."

"Sure. I can do that." He tipped the table over and folded the legs.

Watching him work, Kelly injected exaggerated amazement into her voice. "You play golf? Why I remember Riley whipping you badly on the cruise."

"Hey, that was Putt-Putt." Eric's smile was sheepish. "I see I have yet to live down that humiliating defeat. Actually, I do it more for the fresh air and exercise. I don't use a cart, and I carry my own clubs." He picked up the folded table by the edge with one hand. "Where to?"

"I'm parked out back." They headed through the back room toward the alley. "Carrying clubs sounds like good exercise," Emma said. She revised her image of him tooling around on a cart to walking the greens, a heavy golf bag slung over his shoulder. "You don't even use wheels?"

"Nope. That's cheating. I've got a group of friends who carry too. Super-golf, we call it." He grinned. "The loser gets to carry the refreshments in addition to their clubs on the next round."

Emma lowered the backseat with Kelly's help, and Eric slid the table in. Then he fetched the frame from the back room and placed it in the cargo hold. As Emma shut the hatch, Eric looked at his watch. "Gotta run. Emma, I'll see you tomorrow at church." With a goodbye wave, he strode down the alley.

"I'll be there," she called, feeling herself blush again as Kelly threw her a curious look. "We're having lunch at the country club. That's all, OK?" She moved briskly toward the back door. "Let's figure out what we need for the Tolliver quilt. I loaded the photos."

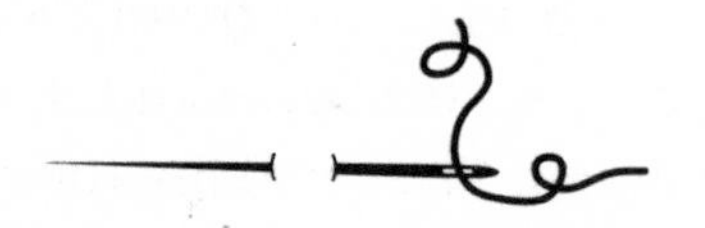

"You're right. They did tear apart your room," Emma said, standing in the doorway of Nate's bedroom, tucked under the eaves on the third floor. It was as she had imagined it: the sheets torn off and flung on the floor, the closet—merely a pole behind a curtain—stripped of clothes, drawers tipped up, contents scattered. Books and papers were sprinkled over the top of the chaos like scholarly confetti. At least they didn't appear to be ripped up.

Kelly nudged her aside a little, peering in to see. "Is anything missing?"

Nate, hovering behind them in the hall with Olivia, snorted. "I have no idea. When I clean it up, I'll find out. Then I'll report the theft to the police. You asked me to wait until you got here, so I did."

"What about your computer?" Emma asked. "I don't see one." The small antique desk was bare. That's what she would have taken, had she been on the trail of the treasure.

"Fortunately, I had it with me. I was at the college library most of the day doing research."

"Well, it'll give you a good chance to clean your room," Olivia said. "It was a mess to begin with."

"That's not funny, Sis."

Olivia's face sagged. "I know. I was just trying to lighten the mood. Everything stinks lately. Listen, I'll go down and make coffee. You all want some?"

"Sure," Emma said. "After we bring in our equipment. Do you mind helping us, Nate? We need to bring in a table and frame from the car so we can set up a workstation for the intarsia quilt. And then we'll be able to fit the net in the Jeep."

"Oh, yeah," Nate said, reluctantly turning away from his destroyed room. "Where are you going to work on the quilt?"

"One of the bedrooms," Emma said. "We'll show you."

They received a shock when they opened the door to the bedroom. The contents of the armoire and bureau had been unceremoniously dumped on the carpet and all over the bed, which remained intact, to Emma's relief. Fortunately, they'd covered the quilt with another drop cloth before leaving.

"Someone's been in here too, obviously." Nate screwed up his face in either disgust or dismay. Emma couldn't tell which.

"I wonder what they were looking for," Kelly said, her voice casual. "We'll have to pick all this up before we can tear down the bed and set up the table and quilt frame."

"You need to move the bed to make room for your equipment, right? Why don't we just stack the mattresses and bed frame against the wall?"

"That sounds easier than moving them out of here," Emma agreed. She handed him the keys to the Jeep. "Do you mind getting the frame for us? One of us will come down and help you lug it up here. We'll get started cleaning this up."

He grabbed the keys, and a moment later they heard his footsteps echoing down the stairs. Kelly dropped the tote, rummaged through it, and pulled out two pairs of white gloves. "We'd better hurry. He won't be gone long."

Emma pulled on gloves and kicked off her shoes before wading through the clothes and linens on the floor, pushing them aside the best she could. It was against her principles to damage vintage textiles by stepping all over them with dirty shoes. She knelt down and thrust her hands under the spread and between the mattress and box spring. "It's still here." Wincing at the thought of handling the soiled garment, she pulled it out.

Kelly was ready, holding an evidence collection bag. "Pop that in here and I'll hide it in the tote until we can figure out what to do with it."

"We have to leave it in the house somewhere. Somewhere no one will find it."

"Or we could call the police."

Emma knew the law-abiding thing to do would be to call Spinelli and report it to him. Maybe they should. They could pretend it had been hidden under the mattress all this time. But then she thought about how the detective had railroaded poor Dottie Faye into an arrest before the medical examiner's report was even complete.

She shook her head decisively. "No. Not yet. When we're ready, the shirt will magically show up in the armoire again, where it was originally left."

"I'm glad you said that. Spinelli is as uncooperative as the Mystic Harbor police. They remind me of a quote I once heard. 'Some people's minds are like concrete: all mixed up and permanently set.'"

"In their case, it's all made up." Emma slid the shirt into the bag, relieved to release it from her hands. Then she stripped off the gloves and tossed them into the tote to dispose of outside the house. "I'll have to put on a new pair when we unearth the quilt from that pile."

Kelly took off her own gloves and set the zipped tote next to the bureau. "I'll go down and help Nate."

Emma picked up clothes from the floor and hung them in the armoire but quickly tired of the effort and piled them inside instead. Someone else could deal with them later. She stuffed the linens back into the bureau, ignoring her natural inclination to fold them perfectly first.

Nate and Kelly left the frame in the hall and went to get the table. Gloved again, Emma and Kelly gently rolled up the quilt in its protective covering of drop cloths and set it carefully in another bedroom for the moment. Working as a team, they stripped the bed and stacked the components against the wall. Then they brought in the table and frame and set them up. The quilt was carried back in and left rolled up for safekeeping until they began the conservation work.

"Let's take a break," Emma suggested.

"Olivia brought some homemade pie from the restaurant," Nate said. "Chocolate cream."

A finger on her chin, Kelly tipped her head back and forth. "Pie before dinner? Should I or shouldn't I?" She nodded firmly. "I shall." She shot Emma a meaningful look. "But before I go down, I need to, ah, use the facilities."

Emma got it. Kelly was going to hide the shirt. "OK. We'll head down. Coming, Nate?"

A few minutes later, Kelly joined them in the kitchen. Nate and Olivia were steadily working their way through slices of oozing, rich chocolate pudding and hand-whipped heavy cream; Emma had taken an obligatory nibble of hers. Kelly poured herself a cup of coffee and sat down to the slice of pie waiting for her. She took a bite and rolled her eyes in appreciation. "You can always tell homemade pie by the crust. This is perfectly tender and flaky. Just slightly sweet." She glanced at Emma and smiled. "If you're not going to eat that ...."

"Kelly Grace!"

Olivia interrupted the friendly parrying. "Josh is a talented cook, that's for sure," she said. "He does it all. From soup to dessert."

Nate scowled at the praise for his ex-girlfriend's new love, but he quickly finished off his pie anyway. Then he gave a discreet belch behind his fist.

"Nate!" Olivia glared a reprimand. "Not at the table."

"Excuse me," Nate said, glaring back.

"I can tell you two are related," Kelly said. "You act just

like my son and daughter." Catching Emma's eye, she glanced at Olivia's fork and cup.

Emma nodded in understanding. Hopefully they would be able to get her DNA from one of them. Or Nate's. She hadn't had a chance to find out if his DNA would be a close enough match to Olivia's to be used as a sample.

"Yeah, we tend to fall back into certain patterns," Olivia admitted. "I guess old habits die hard."

"Like trying to run my life? Yeah, that's a habit that you could work on breaking." Nate cut himself another sliver of pie from what remained.

"That's what people who love you do. No matter how old you are, apparently." Emma smiled at Nate, trying to lighten his mood by showing sympathy.

Olivia sighed. "I guess I got in the habit when our parents died. Nate was just finishing high school." To Emma's dismay, she picked up her plate, fork, and cup and carried them to the counter.

"Was that before you went out West to live?" Emma asked.

Olivia set the plate and fork in the sink and ran water over them. "Yes. After I got him settled at college the first time, I moved to California." After refilling her coffee cup, she returned to the table.

"I thought I wanted to major in geology and then changed my major," Nate said. "So do a lot of people. You're not doing what *you* went to school for."

"That's true. I'm running a restaurant, not designing textiles. Oh, well. That's life," said Olivia.

"Is that what you were majoring in at Hawthorne?" Kelly asked. "Textile design?"

"Yes. Danielle was too. It's a tough field to break into. We can't all be Antonio Roman."

"We use his fabrics all the time. They are spectacular," Kelly agreed. Like Olivia and Danielle, Antonio Roman—known then as Tony Mann—had been one of Rose's students, but DNA results had cleared him.

"The quilt field needs more restoration professionals," Emma said. "You might consider going into that."

"Maybe I will. Right now I've got to figure out what's going to happen to the restaurant. Everything is still up in the air."

Nate grunted a laugh of bitter agreement. "Besides figuring out what I'm going to do about my thesis with Bart gone, I want to find out who messed with my stuff. It's pretty disturbing."

Emma took advantage of the opening to ask him, "Where were you when Bart was killed?"

Nate tipped back in his chair, the two front legs coming off the ground. "Bart sent me on an errand to see someone that morning. But, the weird thing is, the dude wasn't home. So, I have no idea what that was all about."

"That is weird," Emma said. "What do you mean, 'he sent you on an errand?' He told you in person to go?" Maybe Bart had deliberately sent Nate away.

"No. He left me a note. He had a Chamber of Commerce breakfast that morning and they start around seven-thirty, so I was still in bed when he left. After I got up and had coffee, I went to the office, which was my usual routine. We just picked up each day from where we left off the night before."

"What did the note say?" Kelly asked.

Nate shrugged. "Not much. He wanted me to drive over to Obadiah Peabody's and pick up a donation."

"Why would Bart send you out to see someone he knew wasn't home?" Emma mused.

"He wouldn't," Kelly said. "Do you still have the note?"

Nate tipped his chin and peered up at the ceiling, his chair still balancing on the back legs. If he moved too quickly, he would fall right back. To Emma's relief, he reached out one hand and gripped the edge of the table. "I'm trying to remember what I was wearing." He thumped forward. "These shorts." Unsnapping the front cargo pocket, he dug around inside. "And I haven't worn them since, so don't give me that look, Sis. They're still clean." He pulled out a slip of folded paper and passed it over to Emma and Kelly. Indeed it instructed Nate to visit Obadiah. But it was notable for what it didn't reveal.

"This is typed," Emma said. "So we have no idea who actually wrote it."

seventeen

Emma stared at the slip of paper, wishing it were more informative—with a handwriting sample, for example. Nate could have typed it. So could the killer if he had wanted to get Nate out of the way. "Did Bart generally type notes for you?"

Nate shook his head. "No. I thought it was a little odd, but he wasn't there to ask, so I took off."

"What time was that?" Kelly asked.

He scratched his nose. "Um. Around 9:20 or so. It took about twenty minutes to drive out there. Then I stood there on his doorstep for ten banging on the door. Finally, his neighbor came out and told me he was out of town."

"Who was the neighbor?" Emma asked.

"Matilda Bennett. She's also given money to the museum."

Emma thought over the timeline. Their appointment had been for 10 a.m. Bart was dead when they arrived. So, unless Nate killed him before he took off to establish an alibi, Bart died between 9:20 and 10 a.m. "How late do those chamber meetings go?"

Nate shoved back his chair hard, making it scrape across the wooden floors, and jumped to his feet. They all jumped at the sudden move. Olivia gasped.

"I know what you're doing. You're trying to find out if I really have an alibi." Leaning on the table with both hands, he glared at Emma and Kelly.

Her pulse racing, Emma watched him closely. Was he guilty? Was he going to run away or attack them? She glanced around for something to use as a weapon if need be. The most dangerous item on the table was a blunt butter knife that was used to cut the pie.

Olivia reached out a placating hand. "Calm down, Nate. Of course they want to check your alibi. Plus, figuring out where you were when it happened will help narrow down who killed poor Bart." She turned to Emma. "I never believed it was your aunt. Yes, Bart could be a pain, but I doubt she'd drag two witnesses along if she were going to commit murder."

Kelly chuckled. "That's true. Dottie Faye is known for her discretion."

Olivia gave her a funny look while Emma rolled her eyes. Fortunately, Olivia's intervention drained the tension out of Nate like air out of a balloon. With a huge, rattling sigh, he slumped back into his chair. "Go ahead. Check me out. I guess I don't blame you since they're trying to pin it on Dottie Faye."

"Who's in charge of the chamber meetings?" Kelly asked. She sat poised to look up the number in her phone. Nate told her, and while Kelly called the chamber president to find out when the meeting had adjourned, Emma called Matilda. Then, after inquiring into his wrist condition, Emma stepped out of the kitchen and called Eric.

He picked up right away. "Emma. How's it going?"

She heard voices and the clatter of glassware in the background and guessed he was at the county club, probably in the lounge. "Everything's fine. I have a medical question. I hope it's a good time."

"Any time is a good time to hear from you." He laughed. "That sounded dorky, huh? Go ahead, and I'll do my best. If I don't know, maybe one of my friends will. The other guys in my foursome are doctors too."

Emma explained Nate's wrist problem and mentioned the diagnosis he'd been given, a perilunate dislocation.

Eric whistled. "Those are nasty. He'll probably have to have surgery to stabilize the joint."

"In your opinion, would that injury affect use of that hand?"

"It could. You wouldn't want to put too much pressure or strain on it."

"So, stabbing someone would probably be out of the question?"

Eric must have been taking a drink of something because all Emma heard for a minute was the sound of coughing. "Sorry about that," he said when he came back on. "Your question surprised me, and I choked on my ginger ale." He laughed. "I won't ask for details right now, but I will tell you that anyone with that injury would have a hard time using enough force to successfully stab someone. I assume the stabbing was successful?" His tone was wry.

"Unfortunately, yes." Emma thanked Eric and hung up. Leaning against the hallway wall, she thought about what she'd learned. The medical report stated that the killer used their left hand, and according to Eric, Nate couldn't have used that hand to stab Bart. So, either a right-handed person used their left to throw the police off the track or the killer was left-handed. Something niggled at the back of her mind. She'd noticed another left-handed person recently. *Who was it?* After a fruitless attempt to force the memory out of hiding, she gave up and rejoined the others. Maybe it would surface if she didn't try so hard.

Kelly shared what she had learned, information that cleared Nate and confirmed his alibi. Bart left the meeting at around nine-thirty and walked home, about a five-minute jaunt. Matilda, Obadiah's neighbor, said she saw Nate arrive at about the same time. She remembered because she was waiting for her morning talk show to come on.

"I'm glad you realize I'm innocent," Nate said. "Now we just have to figure out who really killed Bart so we can get Dottie Faye off the hook."

"I think it's coming down to one suspect," Emma said. "Priscilla. But she has an alibi."

"She certainly stands to gain the most." Kelly nodded acceptance as Olivia brought around the coffee pot. "Bart left everything to her—except the treasure."

"That's not a surprise," Nate said. "He told me he was going to leave it to charity."

"Did you know he also left half the value to you?" Emma said gently.

Nate's mouth dropped open. "Really?"

"That's so awesome!" Olivia said. "You could pay off all your loans. Make a new start." She burst into tears.

"Assuming we find it, Sis," Nate said.

"Still. Bart was so generous."

Kelly reached into her handbag and pulled out a package of tissues. She pulled a few out and handed them to Olivia, who wiped her eyes, and then dropped the tissues onto the table. With a wink at Emma, Kelly snagged a couple of used ones and slid them into the handbag. Then she excused herself to go to the ladies' room. Emma knew she was going to tuck away the tissues into evidence envelopes. They had Olivia's DNA sample at last.

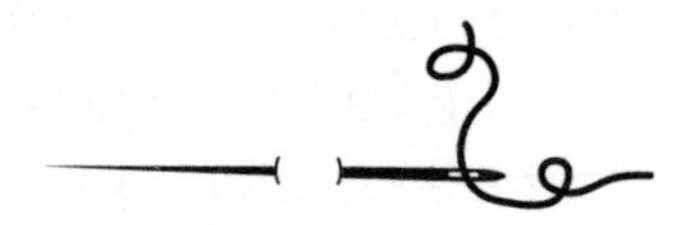

"A little more to the right," Emma said, watching as Eric and Nate made the final adjustments to the potholder quilt decoy Kelly had provided, displayed on a slant board in the back corner of the store. It was the right color and size, so to someone unfamiliar with quilting's finer points, it would pass as the valuable antique.

"Dottie Faye has finished setting up the cameras," Kelly said, emerging from the back room. Infrared cameras were set to record the intruder's entry into the store, placed in the basement and inside the front and back doors. They believed the alley was the most likely avenue of approach but wanted to cover every entrance.

"Be careful," Eric warned as Kelly approached. "If you hit the pressure plate, the net will fall on you."

With a squeak, Kelly stopped short, close to where a pressure plate was hidden under a square of matching carpet. With the help of Eric's special ops friend, Eric and Nate had attached the large, heavy net to the ceiling and connected it to the plate.

"I'll watch from here," Kelly said. Craning her neck, she checked out the setup. "I like how you put the shelves to funnel the prowler into the trap." The way they had arranged the inventory, someone could approach the quilt only through one narrow walkway.

"It almost caught you, didn't it?" Emma said with a laugh. "You were our test."

"I think we're ready to get into position," Nate said. He moved a display slightly and sidled along the wall. Eric and Emma followed, and Eric moved the display back into place.

In the back room, they decided on assignments. Eric waited in his parked car in the alley in case the prowler approached from that direction. In the apartment, Dottie Faye monitored and recorded camera feeds. Nate, Emma, and Kelly took positions in the store, hunkered down behind tall shelves. All had cellphones set on silent so they could communicate via text. The lights were off, the only illumination provided by a streetlight shining through the tall front windows.

"I hope he comes tonight," Emma said. She sat cross-legged behind a display of bolted fabrics, which emitted a pleasant odor of sized cotton. "Otherwise all this effort is for nothing."

"The president sounded overly interested when I called," Kelly said, from her position across the store, near the diaper bags. "He asked me twice when the VIP event was. He also wanted to know about the quilt and how valuable and rare it was."

"I'm so glad we used a decoy." Emma shuddered. "I don't want the potholder quilt anywhere near our prowler."

"Thanks for including me," Nate said. Behind a bookshelf, he sat closest to the quilt where he could help ensure the prowler remained trapped. "This is kind of fun."

"It feels good to do something," Emma admitted. "This person has been harassing us for almost a year."

They fell silent and Emma allowed her mind to wander to more pleasant topics. Earlier that day she and Eric had gone to the country club as planned and enjoyed a wonderful meal. Sitting under an umbrella next to the pool, sipping a glass of white wine and eating blackened shrimp salad, she had glimpsed a life full of pleasure and free from care. Guilt had quickly risen up, of course. Rose was denied a full span of years, the opportunity to fall in love and have a family. How could Emma be allowed to enjoy them if Rose couldn't? She recognized these feelings as survivor's guilt. But the label unfortunately didn't erase them entirely.

Please, Emma. Love your life. Live it fully. Otherwise they killed us both.

Emma jumped. She must have fallen asleep and imagined Rose's words. But even if they were a dream, she felt comforted. Rose probably would say something like that.

A text flashed on her phone. Eric. *He's here.* As expected, the prowler had approached the rear of the store. From an electric shift she sensed in the silent darkness, she knew Kelly and Nate had gotten the message too.

Straining her ears, she thought she heard faint scratching at the rear door. The door groaned open and shut with a soft thud. Footsteps creaked across the wooden floor of the back room. A penlight flashed a slender beam around the store as he entered, touching the ceiling, the shelves of inventory, and the carpet. Peering through a space between two bolts of cloth, Emma saw a figure dressed entirely in black, including face mask and gloves.

Clapping a hand over her mouth, she bit her lip, trying to choke off any possible noise she might make.

The ever mysterious and elusive stalker was here in the store, right in front of her. The person responsible for causing them constant fear and anxiety crept across the rug, flashlight sweeping as he sought what he believed was a rare and valuable antique. So he could damage them yet again.

Emma filled with rage, and she had to clench her fists to prevent herself from flying at him. How dare he torment them? The incidents rushed through her mind like scenes from a horror movie. This monster had even tried to kill Ichabod, an innocent kitten. Now that the situation was close to resolution, she trembled at the burden of what they had endured. His relentless evil had penetrated every part of their lives like a miasma of poisonous fog.

The intruder lifted something he held at his side. A silver canister. Taking another step forward, he aimed the canister and pressed the button. Emma realized it was a can of spray paint. It would have destroyed the potholder quilt beyond repair.

Thump! "What the—" The heavy net fell from the ceiling

and landed on the prowler, bearing him to the ground under its weight.

With a war whoop, Nate dashed from his hiding place and tackled the man, now rolling, thrashing, and yelling in the net. Eric burst into the store and joined him. Kelly flicked on the overhead lights. Dottie Faye ran down the stairs from the apartment, phone in hand, calling 911.

"Want to do the honors, Emma?" Eric asked, nodding toward the face mask. He sat on the man's chest and arms while Nate pinned his legs. The man twisted, trying to dislodge Eric and Nate. "Cut it out. It's over. The police are on their way."

Emma pushed the net away from the man's face. She grabbed the bottom of the mask at the neck and tugged. He yelled as the woolen mask pulled over his chin and nose but she kept tugging, gradually revealing his face.

Sitting back, Emma realized with a stab of disappointment that he wasn't President Coleman or former Chief Harry Moran. He looked familiar, but she couldn't place him. Had they been wrong in their assumptions about the prowler? But only the chief and president were invited for tomorrow.

"That's Russ Jones," Dottie Faye said. "The janitor from the college."

Now Emma remembered him. He had cleaned up Dottie Faye's spilled coffee the day they visited Hawthorne College. "Who put you up to this?" she asked.

"I'm not talking." He grunted. "Can you guys get up? You're killing me."

"Only if you stay put," Eric said. At Russ's nod, he got up, as did Nate. They stood close by, ready to tackle the man again should it be required.

Russ sat up and pushed the net off his upper body. He rubbed his arms, grumbling.

"Who sent you here?" Emma asked.

"I'm not talking," he said again, flexing his legs.

Kelly hunkered down, staring right into his face. "So, you're going to take the rap? Even if someone else planned everything?" She shook her head. "Not too smart."

"Yeah, you might be able to make a deal," Eric said. "Maybe you'll even get off with probation." He smiled sadly. "Otherwise you're going away for a long, long time."

Confusion followed by fear flashed over the janitor's face. "I didn't plan anything. I just followed orders. I swear. None of this was my idea. They told me I'd be fired if I didn't go along with it. It was all Coleman and Moran."

A jangling tone rang from Russ's jacket pocket. Without asking for permission, Nate bent down and fished inside, pulling out a cellphone. He displayed the name on the screen to everyone.

Harry Moran.

Nate answered, flicking it onto speakerphone as he did so. "Hello?"

"How'd it go?" The chief's gruff voice projected loud and clear over the speaker.

Nate grinned. "Great. Pick me up at the jail."

eighteen

"How was your night, Emma?" Kelly called out as she entered Cotton & Grace carrying two large pizzas. A savory odor of tomato sauce and melted cheese wafted from the boxes.

Emma stretched as she got up from the design desk. She'd taken advantage of the quiet morning to examine the photos of the intarsia quilt again and double-check the list of what they needed for the conservation job. "I slept better than I have in ages. I guess I didn't realize how much I worried about the prowler until he was gone."

"Same here." Kelly slid the pizzas onto the counter after Emma cleared away the paperwork. "I think I was sleeping with one eye open all this time." The store was closed today, but they were meeting to take care of other business—trapping a killer and locating a treasure.

Dottie Faye pushed through the door, carrying an insulated container of iced tea. "Good afternoon, girls." She set down the tea beside the pizza boxes. "This is my homemade tea with about half the sugar I usually put in." Rooting around in her capacious handbag, white sailcloth trimmed with blue piping, she pulled out a handful of sugar packets. She laughed. "I still can't get over how that Russ sang like a canary last night. Talk about sweet justice."

The shop phone rang and Emma answered. "No comment," was her only comment before hanging up. "Another reporter," she explained. "They've been calling all morning."

Dottie Faye reached into her bag and pulled out a local

newspaper. "College President and Former Police Chief Questioned in Prowler Case," the headline screamed in bold typeface. "It's all over the news too. I saw a story on that station out of Boston."

"I hope they nail them," Kelly said. "We'll have to testify, I'm sure, but it will be worth it."

Kelly fetched paper plates and napkins from the back room and they all dug in, grabbing hot slices of pizza loaded with veggies and extra cheese.

"The look on Tom Boyer's face was priceless," Emma said with a smile of satisfaction. Once the janitor realized that he was going to pay for his crimes, he'd made sure to tell the deputy chief that he was only following orders. Emma had thoroughly enjoyed being vindicated and telling Boyer that smoke generally meant fire. In other words, why would Coleman and Moran go to such lengths unless there was indeed something to cover up in Rose's death? Boyer hadn't said much, but Emma could tell by his disconcerted expression that she was on the right track. By the looks of it, the media wasn't going to let the prowler's connection to the college rest, either.

Dottie Faye poured paper cups of tea and handed them around. Kelly lifted hers. "A toast. To a mystery solved." They touched cups. "We need to savor our victory because we still have a lot of work to do."

"Speaking of which, did you hear back from the lab yet?" Emma asked.

"We should hear this afternoon." Dottie Faye glanced at the wall clock. "And Nate should be here any minute to help us figure out where the treasure is hidden."

"He better hurry before the pizza's gone," Kelly said, grabbing another slice. A tapping on the front door attracted their attention. "There he is now." Nate stood at the door, a manila envelope under his arm.

After lunch, they went upstairs to the apartment and laid out the tunnel map on the table Eric had carted up there, since that was the only surface large enough. Their other table was at the Tolliver mansion.

"I'm so glad Bart gave you a copy of the map, Dottie Faye," Nate said. "Otherwise, we'd be totally sunk. Did he give you the clue too?"

"He sure did. And except for when I was carted off to jail, it hasn't been off my person." Dottie Faye unclasped the compass rose necklace Bart had given her. Then she unfastened the locket case and extracted the slip of paper hidden there. She handed it to Nate. "I hope you can make more sense out of this than I can."

"'The seventh step in the seventh gate,'" he read. "Hmm. From Benjamin Tolliver's hints, I firmly believe that the treasure was hidden down there. But I've never seen any steps in the tunnel itself."

"How about where it connects to the house?" Emma leaned over the map, pointing to where the tunnel intersected the Tolliver mansion's basement. "Maybe the gate is the door."

Nate shook his head. "There are only one or two steps down into the tunnel, not seven. At the other end, on the waterfront, there was a slope so loaded carts could be pushed up toward the house or another destination." He ran his finger down the tunnel to the docks. "The tunnel stops about here on the other side of Water Street since someone who renovated the dockside warehouse blocked it off. It's part of their basement now."

"I sure hope it wasn't hidden at that end," Kelly said.

"They might have found it during the renovations, then," Dottie Faye said.

"I never heard that they did, and that treasure is too notable to remain a secret." Nate unfastened the clasp on the manila envelope and spread a series of color photographs on the table. "Here are some pictures from inside the tunnel."

Picking one up, Emma studied the tunnel made of bricks and intersected by reinforcing archways every so many feet. "What if those are the gates? The arches?" She handed the photo to Nate.

"Hmm. Maybe. A bit of a stretch." He put the picture on the table and stared at it as though it might yield answers.

Kelly searched the Internet on her phone. "One definition of gate is opening."

"In that case, the clue might mean doors or doorways." Nate bent over the map and counted. "But there are only two openings into the tunnel before it reaches the Tolliver mansion."

Emma got the tingling feeling that meant she was on to something significant. "I really think I'm right. Benjamin wouldn't have wanted it to be too obvious, right?" She traced one of the arches in the photo. "Many gates are an arched shape."

"What about the steps, then?" Nate stilled looked skeptical.

She jabbed a finger at the double stacks of bricks forming the bottom of the arches. They jutted out slightly. "See how they're offset? Those are the steps, I bet."

"You could be right," Nate said. "Now it's a matter of figuring out which arch is the right one. I'm going to assume it's the seventh one up from the waterfront."

"But some at that end are missing," Kelly said. "Buried, you said."

Nate winked and pulled a pen out of his pocket. "Got a piece of paper? I know about how far apart they are. So, I'll measure up from the docks and see where it brings us."

Emma found a scrap of paper, and Nate made his

calculations, referring to the scale of the map. "I'm guessing it should be right here." He pointed to the spot just up from where the Tolliver tunnel crossed Water Street. "We're in luck. That piece of the tunnel is still intact."

Dottie Faye clapped her hands. "I knew y'all would figure it out. Bart would be so proud. So, how soon can we get down there and find that little ol' treasure?"

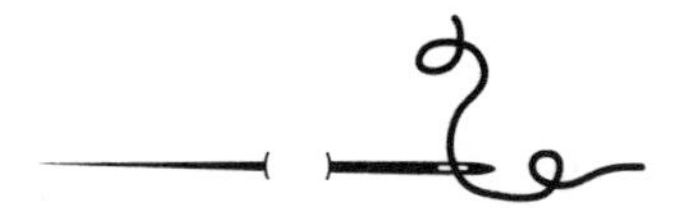

Emma knocked on the metal back door of the Crow's Nest Café, located in the dead-end alley between the restaurant and a souvenir shop. She looked around at the dumpsters and piled boxes crowding the narrow space, the smell of garbage strong in the hot summer night air. "I hope we're in the right place."

"This is where Nate said to meet him," Kelly said.

"Want me to go back to the street and see if I can spot him?" Eric offered. He had joined the trio in Lantern Cove on the mission to find the treasure.

Emma was about to say yes when the door swung open with a rattle. Nate wore his usual flannel shirt and jeans, with the jaunty addition of a climbing lamp clasped around his head, like a miner. "Hey. Did you bring flashlights?" He touched his headgear. "Or these?" He stepped back so they could enter.

"Everyone has their own light," Emma said. "And we brought extra batteries, just in case." Emma didn't relish going into a tight, dark space underground. If there wasn't a treasure involved, practically nothing on earth could have induced her to join this expedition.

The kitchen was dark and quiet, the dishes all washed and stacked and the grills scraped clean. An odor of cleaning products hung in the air. Kelly set down her tote and pulled out flashlights.

"How do we get to the tunnel?" Eric asked, glancing around curiously. "It's amazing that they connect all over town."

Nate slung an old canvas knapsack over his shoulder and led the way to a door in the corner. "Down in the basement. The Water Street tunnel will lead us to the Tolliver tunnel. Eventually."

Dottie Faye adjusted the combination lantern and video camera she wore strapped on her head, her blond hair puffing out above and below. "How far is it?"

"A couple of blocks." Nate switched on a light and they followed him down a narrow set of wooden steps to the dirt-floored basement. Cobwebs were strung between the rafters. The only things in the dank space were a huge old furnace, water heater, and empty shelves. "Olivia doesn't use the basement for much, as you can see. It's too damp and dirty to store anything."

Taking a sniff of the musty air, Emma silently agreed that it wouldn't be a good place to store even sealed cans and bottles. "You're sure the tunnel is open all the way?" She pictured cave-ins blocking the way. Or one happening while they were in there, tons of bricks and dirt and rocks falling on their heads, filling the air with clouds of choking dust. Maybe this wasn't such a good idea.

Nate shoved aside one of the empty shelving units, helped by Eric. "I'm positive. I've been down there fairly often over the past few months. The remaining tunnels are in good condition. They were built to last."

Behind the shelves was a tall wooden door with a brass knob. Nate glanced at each of them in turn. "Ready?" He opened the door, the knob turning easily. Cool air smelling of ancient dust and the sea rushed at their faces.

"Where does the air come from?" Eric asked. "I thought it would be stuffy down here." His voice echoed in the hollow space.

"There are openings up to the street. They let in fresh air." Nate switched on his lamp and stepped into the tunnel, turning right—which was north—toward the Tolliver house. Dottie Faye and Kelly followed. Their flashlight beams revealed an arched brick enclosure just over seven feet high. The floor, also laid with bricks, was strewn with rubble.

Emma hesitated on the threshold, her stomach clenched. Her feet felt glued to the ground and she literally could not lift her leg to make the first step. She tried to tell herself it was no worse than going on a subway train but somehow her body wasn't getting the message. Maybe because it was so dark, their puny beams the only bulwark against utter and total darkness.

Eric noticed her distress. "How about I walk beside you, Emma?" He leaned close and whispered, "I don't like the idea of going underground, either."

She didn't really believe him, but his support made moving possible, and they stepped into the tunnel. Shining their lights on the ground, they cautiously proceeded, careful not to turn an ankle on a stray brick or stone.

"That must go into another building," Eric said, pointing his light at an arched opening in the side of the tunnel. His light picked out a doorknob, dull with dust. "I wonder how many people know their businesses are connected this way."

"From what Nate said, just about everyone moved around down here at one time." Emma was starting to relax. So far nothing terrible had happened, and she hadn't seen any rats or other nasty creatures.

"It must have been handy in the winter, that's for sure."

"Especially since they didn't plow the streets. Better than shoveling." In the old days, Emma knew they sometimes rolled or plowed the snow with horse-drawn equipment. Otherwise, travel was often impeded for months when the snow was deep.

Eric pointed his light straight up. "See those squares? Those are glass blocks set in the sidewalk. I've seen those walking down the street and never thought anything of it. They must let a little light in during the day."

"This is like stepping back in time. It's really quite interesting." Emma shined her light around to see what she could discover and caught something dark lying next to the wall. With a jump of her pulse, she wondered if it was a dead animal. "Um, Eric. What's that?" She held her light on the shape.

Without displaying any qualms, he marched toward the lump, shining his own light on it. He bent and picked it up. Emma cringed and shut her eyes, fearing to see something disgusting. Noticing her reaction, he laughed. "It's a hat. Look." He twirled it around on his hand. "It's in good condition, so it can't have been down here long." He sniffed it. "It even smells clean."

Emma realized that the hat was a navy blue poke bonnet, very similar to the ones Priscilla wore. *How did that get down here?*

Playing around, Eric tried to place it on her head. "You want it?"

She stepped back, ducking her head away. "I do. But don't put it on me. It might be evidence."

"Really? What should I do with it?"

Emma hated to let it out of her sight, fearing they might never find it again or the person who left it might come to retrieve it. "Hold on to it for now."

"Hey, guys. Where are you?" Nate yelled from up ahead.

"We're coming," Emma called back. Eric held the bonnet by the strings, and they hastened to catch up. Their friends stood at the junction of another tunnel, which ran perpendicular to the one they were in.

"This is the Tolliver tunnel," Nate said. He pointed right. "The waterfront is down there." Left. "And the house up there."

"What's that?" Dottie Faye asked, catching sight of the bonnet swinging from Eric's hand.

"We found it," Emma said. "It looks just like Priscilla's bonnet."

"Can I see that?" Kelly asked. Eric handed the bonnet to her, and she peered closely at it. "You're right. But what was it doing down there? Does Priscilla go to the café that way?"

"I don't think so," Nate said. "And if she did, she wouldn't leave her bonnet behind." He snorted. "She's very fussy about her costumes."

"I'm thinking someone else wore it," Emma said. "Someone pretending to be Priscilla."

"What do you mean?" Dottie Faye pursed her lips, puzzled. "Who would want to pretend to be that sour old thing?"

Kelly snapped her fingers. "I get it. The bank. The teller said Priscilla had worn her costume in the drive-through the day Bart was killed. What if it was someone else posing as Priscilla?"

"There goes her alibi," Emma said.

"Wow. All that from a hat." The bonnet back in his hand, Eric stared at it in amazement.

"These girls are good," Dottie Faye said. She tapped her headlamp. "And I'm getting every minute of it on film."

Nate shifted from foot to foot. "This is all great work, but let's go see if that treasure is where I think it is. I'm dying to find out."

"Yes, onward to the treasure!" Kelly cried. Over her shoulder, she added with a laugh, "Take good care of that bonnet, Eric."

"Please do," Dottie Faye said. "You could be holding the proof of my innocence."

Nate led the way into the Tolliver tunnel, which was slightly narrower and with a lower ceiling, probably because it wasn't a main thoroughfare like the Water Street tunnel, Emma concluded.

"According to my calculations, it's the first archway after the intersection," Nate muttered. He found the spot and stopped, taking his backpack off and dropping it with a clatter of metal. "Here we are." As the others gathered around, he opened the pack and pulled out a chisel, mason's hammer, and crow bar.

"What do we need those for?" Emma asked.

"I'm thinking he might have mortared in the treasure," Nate said, crouching down to examine the bricks. "But it won't be exactly the same texture or color, since it was done at a different time." He pointed to the other side of the arch. "Why don't a couple of you look on that side?"

Dottie Faye took over bonnet duty so Eric could help Nate check bricks. Kelly and Emma did the same on the other end of the arch.

"First let's count seven layers up," Kelly said. "I'll start on one side and you do the other."

Emma noticed the main mortar color was gray and rather crumbly with drips and globs that spoke of hasty construction. But right in the corner next to the tunnel wall, the last brick was grouted with a finer, almost yellow mortar. It made sense that Benjamin would tuck a secret compartment out of sight of any casual passerby.

"I think I found it." She grabbed the brick and wiggled. It was tightly cemented in place. "But we'll need those tools."

Nate brought over the hammer and chisel and got to work. Within minutes the old mortar gave way and the brick dropped out, revealing an opening. He put the tools down and sat back on his heels. "I'm almost afraid to reach in there. People have been looking for this since 1787." His breathless laugh mingled disbelief and excitement.

"Go on, Nate," Dottie Faye urged. "You've earned it with all the help you gave Bart."

"Can you get that chamois cloth out of my pack and set it on the ground?" he asked Kelly. She complied, and as Nate slowly reached his hand into the hole, Emma held her breath. He groped around inside. "There's something here." He pulled out a black leather bag and placed it reverently on the cloth.

Everyone stared at it for a moment. Then Nate carefully opened the sack and slid the contents onto the cloth. Even in the dim artificial light of the lamps and torches, diamonds and emeralds flashed their brilliant fire for the first time in hundreds of years.

nineteen

"The treasure is real," Nate said, amazement in his voice. "Old Benjamin Tolliver wasn't lying." He gently pulled the intricate necklace into position, demonstrating how it would look draped around a woman's neck. A large emerald—about the size of a robin's egg—was the centerpiece. Smaller emeralds, three on each side, were attached to the main chain by diamond flower shapes. Each emerald was edged with even more diamonds.

"It's gorgeous." Emma stroked the largest gem with one finger. "I'm not really a jewelry person, but I can understand why someone would love that necklace."

Dottie Faye purred in agreement. "It's stunning. I can just see it with a black velvet gown." She ran her hands across her chest as though imagining how it would look.

Kelly gave a huge sigh. "A queen or empress must have owned that. It's fit for a crown jewels collection."

The ever-practical Eric asked, "Is there anything else in the bag?"

Nate picked it up with both hands, careful not to stress the ancient leather, and tipped it up. A dozen or more gold coins poured out onto the cloth. By their slightly irregular shape and dull color, Emma guessed they were ancient. "Bart's got a coin guide. We'll have to look these up. But they look Roman." He held one up between two fingers. "This looks like a medallion. They're very rare."

"How rare?" Dottie Faye asked.

Nate gulped. "I don't even want to say. But they've sold for seven figures."

Eric whistled. "Wow."

As the excitement of finding the fabled cache ebbed, unease walked cold fingers up Emma's neck. Someone else wanted these jewels and coins, and they'd killed once in the quest to find them already. "We really should get out of here. And we need to put your inheritance somewhere secure for safekeeping, Nate."

Nate picked up the necklace and slid it back into the bag. "Where do you suggest? The bank won't be open until tomorrow morning." He looked around the dark tunnel. "I'd hate to leave it down here in case Priscilla or someone else stumbles on it. And the same thing could happen if I take it to my room in the mansion. Someone already searched it once."

And if Priscilla is the killer, you certainly don't want to stay there.

"We have a safe at the store," Emma said. "And you can sleep in the apartment tonight so you'll be close by your treasure at all times until you get to the bank."

"Great idea, Emma," Kelly said. "No one will even know you're there, Nate. Thanks to you and Eric, the prowler is now in jail, so you should have a nice quiet night."

"They'll all be quiet once we catch Bart's killer," Nate said. He wrapped the leather bag in the chamois cloth and placed it carefully in the front zipper pouch of his pack. Then he set the brick carefully back into place, packing the crumbled mortar around it. "Not perfect, but it should fool a casual eye."

"I have an idea how we can trap the killer," Emma said. "Let's meet tomorrow and talk about it." She pointed at the bonnet Dottie Faye held. "Bring that with you."

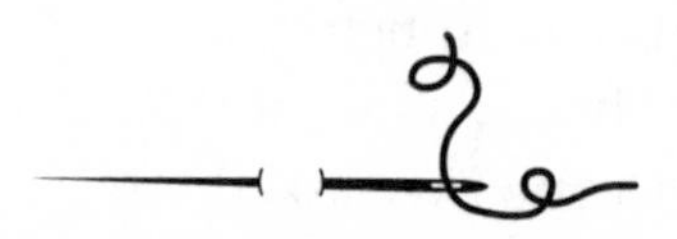

"What's this?" Cortland Cabot asked, staring at the blue bonnet in a clear evidence bag sitting in the middle of his enormous polished desk.

"That's some of the evidence we have that will clear Dottie Faye," Emma said, sitting in the client chair next to her aunt. Kelly sat on Dottie Faye's other side. Emma went on to explain where they'd found it. "It has something to do with Bart's murder, I just know it."

"We think the killer is Priscilla Tolliver," Kelly said. "She's the one who gains the most from his death. We checked out Nate's alibi, and he's innocent."

Cortland shook his head as though clearing his ears. "You checked out Nate's alibi?"

"We think Priscilla wore Nate's shirt to do the deed," Dottie Faye said. "I bet that skinny little Yankee weasel was planning to frame him. Then I showed up on the scene and made a much better fall guy."

"Whoa." The attorney held up a hand. "What's this about Nate's shirt? He's the student who was living in the mansion, right?"

Emma explained how they'd found a bloodstained flannel shirt in an armoire filled with vintage clothing in the spare bedroom.

"Where's the shirt now?"

"We left it there. We didn't want to tamper with evidence. But we hid it somewhere safe so it wouldn't disappear."

Cortland groaned. "You could consider that tampering. Why didn't you call the police? Or me?" He rubbed one hand over his face.

Emma shrugged. "They'd just say Dottie Faye wore it. Don't worry, we're going to put the shirt back where we found it and then tell the police."

By the look on his face, Emma expected him to put his fingers in his ears and sing, "La, la, la. I don't want to hear this." Instead, he said, "This is all interesting, but I don't think it's quite enough to get them to drop the charges. There's no proof the bonnet is related to the crime. And you're right, the shirt could have been worn by anyone, including Dottie Faye."

"What if one of Priscilla's hairs is on it?" Kelly asked.

"You found it in a wardrobe full of her clothes, right? They could argue it picked it up then."

"What about Priscilla being left-handed?" Emma asked. She had finally remembered the other left-handed person she'd recently seen. In the altercation at the café, Priscilla had slapped Dottie Faye on the right cheek—with her left hand. "The medical examiner said the killer used his left hand."

"Circumstantial, I'm afraid." He shook his head. "No, I'm afraid we don't have anything conclusive to exonerate Dottie Faye yet. But we might be able to cast doubt. That's really all we need to do."

"Perhaps that's all we *need* to do," Dottie Faye said, rising majestically to her feet, shod in Italian leather stiletto heels. "But I'm not going to stop working until my name is cleared one hundred percent." She leaned across the desk. "I hope you're with me on that, Cortland."

He rose also and came around the desk to usher them out. "Of course. We haven't yet begun to fight."

"That's so true," Dottie Faye said. "Isn't it, girls?"

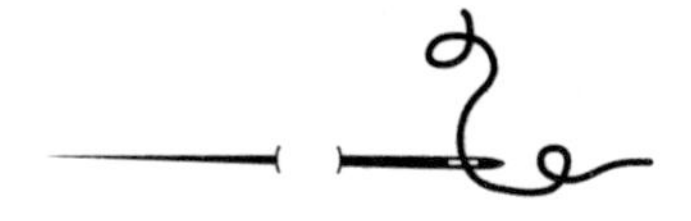

"There he is," Kelly said as Eric entered the Crow's Nest, glanced around, and came toward the booth where she sat with Dottie Faye, Nate, and Emma. They had been waiting for him to arrive before ordering lunch to fuel their "council of war" as Dottie Faye called it.

"He's looking fine. As usual," Dottie Faye said, shooting Emma a sly glance. "It's been nice seeing him so often."

Emma resolutely refused to acknowledge her aunt's comments, but silently she agreed. Eric looked just as good in faded T-shirt, jeans, and sneakers, suitable for tunnel exploring, as he did in everything else he wore. And she had to admit—she did enjoy his company. She waved a hand as Eric approached. "Glad you could make it."

Setting his car keys on the table, he slid in beside Emma. "Me too. I wouldn't miss this for anything. I managed to squeeze in quite a few patients this morning and rescheduled all the non-emergencies."

Sarah brought him a glass of water and stood ready to take their orders, pad and pencil in hand.

He picked up one of the laminated menus. "So, what's good here?"

"Everything," Kelly said. "I'll have the tuna melt, please. On marble pumpernickel."

"I think I'll get a fried clam roll," Eric said. "I haven't had one yet this year."

"They're great here," Nate said. "Especially with onion rings."

"Oh, yeah. Onion rings make it." Eric slapped the menu down. "Thanks."

"Maybe I'll take up super-golf," Emma grumbled, "if it means you don't have to watch what you eat. A shrimp salad for me, please. Light ranch dressing on the side."

Dottie Faye ordered the tuna melt too, and after Sarah left, she said, "Tell us your plan, Emma."

"First I'll tell you my conclusions, and you all tell me if

you agree with them." At their nods, she continued. "The map was stolen. That was a clue that Bart's death wasn't just because Priscilla wanted to inherit sooner rather than later. Only one other person knew about the treasure, and that's you, Nate. When we found the shirt, that was either evidence that Nate did it—"

"What shirt?" Nate asked in a strangled voice.

Kelly glanced at Emma. "Oops. I guess we didn't tell you." Speaking quietly, Kelly told Nate about finding and hiding the shirt and their belief that it was worn to implicate him in Bart's death.

Nate slumped back in his seat, his expression stunned. "That ... witch. She was trying to frame me. She has to be the one who sent me on that wild-goose chase to see Obadiah."

"Obadiah Peabody?" Dottie Faye asked. At his nod, she added, "Bart knew that Obadiah was going out of town. Obadiah told us both when he gave us his donation for the museum."

"That confirms your theory, Nate," Emma said. "And explains the typed note."

Nate snapped his fingers. "And that's why she—or someone—trashed my room. They were looking for that shirt after you moved it."

"That's what I think," Emma said. "I haven't quite figured out how she set up that alibi. But I'm convinced she's guilty. So, what we need to do is set a trap. The bait is the treasure." She pointed at Dottie Faye. "And you're going to spring the trap."

Dottie Faye cackled in glee. "Bring it on, sweet pea."

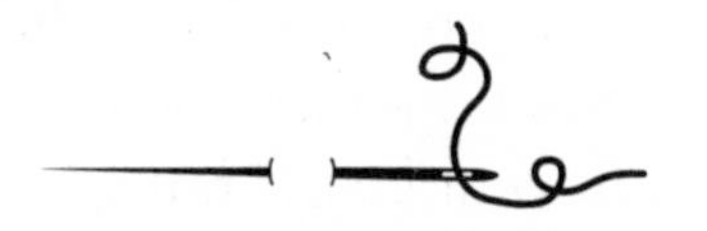

"This quilt really is fabulous," Kelly said, tweaking the intarsia heirloom into place on the frame. "Too bad we probably won't get to finish working on it."

"You're right, it is too bad." Emma pulled a package of sheer silk crepeline mesh out of their supply bag. The fine mesh was applied on top of frayed and damaged fabric to stabilize it.

Kelly laid a section of fiberglass screen over the quilt and ran a hand vacuum cleaner above the screen just close enough to gather dust and dirt.

Priscilla Tolliver pushed through the door, a cellphone clutched in her hand. "What are you doing?" she yelled over the noise of the vacuum.

Kelly switched it off. "I'm gently cleaning the surface. See? Not even touching it. Then Emma and I will add stabilizing mesh to these areas." She pointed to several spots. At Priscilla's skeptical frown, she added, "You won't even notice it."

The older woman sighed deeply. "I guess I'll have to trust you."

"That's what you pay us for," Emma said lightly.

Priscilla's cell rang, a ponderous classical tune. Kelly winked at Emma. Dottie Faye calling right on time.

"Hello? Who is this?" Priscilla walked out of the room and down the hallway. "The map? What makes you think ..."

"The bait is placed," Emma murmured. "Let the games begin."

"The game of mousetrap?" Kelly said with a grin.

"More like rat trap." Emma laid the scaled tissue patterns she'd printed on top of the crepeline. She might as well do something productive while waiting for the meeting Dottie Faye was scheduling with Priscilla. Right now, Eric and Nate were in the tunnel setting up a camera and recording device and replacing the treasure with fake jewels and coins in a leather bag they'd distressed and battered.

Kelly switched on the vacuum and Emma bent over her work, tracing and cutting scraps of fabric. As always, working on a beautiful, fragile piece of history helped her forget the rest of the world for a while.

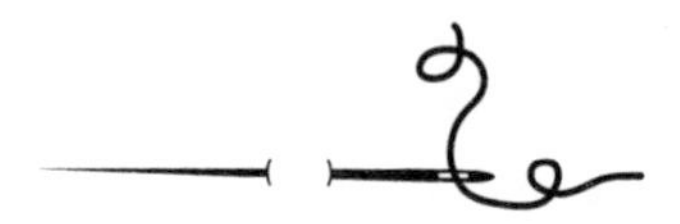

"I think I'm getting used to being down here," Emma whispered. She was hiding with Nate, Eric, and Kelly in a dogleg, a cul-de-sac used to allow the passage of traffic both ways in the tunnel. Around the corner in the Tolliver tunnel, the loose brick was in place for Dottie Faye to "discover."

"We'll have to turn off the lights when they come down," Nate warned. "We don't want any light leakage into that tunnel to tip off Priscilla."

"I guess I can stand it for a few minutes." Emma jostled from foot to foot. "I can't wait for this to all be over."

"You and me both," Kelly said.

Eric made adjustments on his tablet computer. "How's this look?" The others crowded around to see the faintly greenish view of the seventh arch provided by the night camera.

"Not bad," Nate said. "We'll be able to see even more when Dottie Faye and Priscilla bring lights down." He gave Emma a concerned look, his face serious under his headlamp. "Are you sure she'll be all right?"

"If there's one thing I'm sure of, it's that Dottie Faye can handle herself."

"Amen to that." Kelly laughed. "She gives us lessons."

"I might have to take that back," Emma said. "It looks

like they're coming from the wrong direction." She pointed down the Water Street tunnel where a small light bobbed along, aimed at the floor.

"Quick. Douse your lights." Nate reached up and switched off his headlamp. The rest of them copied him and then waited, holding their breath.

"There's only one person," Eric whispered. "I can tell by the footsteps."

Emma strained her ears, listening harder than she ever had in her life. Feet scuffed and shuffled along, occasionally kicking a loose rock. Obviously, the person wasn't afraid of being heard. As the figure drew closer, other sounds drifted toward them.

"They're crying," Emma whispered. "Listen." Low whimpering noises of frustration and despair were clearly heard.

Nate switched on his headlamp and stepped into the tunnel. His light fell directly on a woman's face.

Mandy, the waitress from the café, threw up a hand to block the light. She screamed and jumped back.

"It's me—Nate," he said, stepping closer.

"You scared me." She wiped one hand under her eyes. "What are you doing here?"

He stepped closer. "I have a good reason. It's part of my research for my thesis. Why are you here?"

"I'm looking for something, all right? You're not the only one who's allowed down here. I dropped something the other day, and I came down to find it." Her face twisted as she scanned the floor. "I'm going to be in so much trouble."

Another piece clicked into place for Emma. To test her theory, she stepped out of the alcove, holding the bag containing the blue bonnet. Standing beside Nate, she turned on her flashlight and shined it on the bag. "Is this what you lost, by chance?"

Even in the dim light of the tunnel, Emma saw Mandy's face drain of color. "Where did you get that?"

"We found it down here. Isn't that right, Eric?"

He stepped out to join them. "Yes, we did."

"How many of you are there?" Mandy asked.

"I'm the last," Kelly said, joining the group.

Emma shook the bonnet at Mandy. "I have a theory. I think you wore this bonnet to go to the bank the day Bart was murdered. The teller saw someone in a bonnet and assumed it was Priscilla." She pointed with her flashlight the route she was sure Mandy had taken. "You went from the café to Priscilla's house through the tunnel. Then you drove her car to the bank. After that, you came back through here to the café. That's why you were late that day. Am I'm right?"

Mandy's shoulders drooped, and she ducked her head.

"Why'd you do it, Mandy?" Nate asked, his voice gentle. "Now you're an accessory to murder."

Mandy raised her head, eyes blazing. "I didn't know she was going to kill Bart, I swear. She told me that if I helped her, she would get the restaurant back from Olivia and let Josh run it again."

"And you had no idea how she would make that happen?" Kelly's voice was skeptical.

"I swear," the waitress said again. "She didn't tell me anything."

In the dogleg, the microphone crackled to life. "This is so exciting," Dottie Faye said. "I've never been in a tunnel."

Priscilla grunted. "They're not so exciting after the first dozen times you're down here. So, you think the treasure is right down here, huh?"

"It's time," Nate whispered. "Come on." He grabbed

Mandy's arm. "Come with us. And keep quiet." He tugged her into the alcove.

Eric turned down the microphone feed, and they clustered around, listening intently.

"What are you doing?" Mandy asked.

"Catching a killer," Emma said. "And it might behoove you to cooperate."

"Everything is working out great," Dottie Faye said. "You had the map, and I had the clue ... talk about a partnership." She paused. "'Course it wasn't too smart to take the map without getting the clue. Kinda dead in the water, weren't you?"

Priscilla gave a fake laugh. "I suppose so. I thought Bart had written the clue on the map. What did it say, again?"

Dottie laughed herself. "I haven't told you yet." Another pause. "Before we find the treasure, divvy it up, and go our separate ways, I'd like to know something. Just for my own information. You killed Bart, didn't you?"

"Yes, I did." Priscilla sighed. "I had to. He was going to give his whole estate to his charity." She said "charity" like it was a dirty word.

"I know. I was trying to marry him before he could do that. Bart Tolliver was a fool."

"Good thing you didn't marry him. I would have had to kill both of you." Priscilla's creepy laugh pealed out again. "Just joking."

"Here we are. I think this is the spot." The video feed showed Dottie Faye and Priscilla standing beside the seventh arch.

"Really?" Priscilla twisted back and forth, staring as if the treasure was going to jump out at them.

Dottie Faye set down a camping lantern and crouched in front of the loose brick.

"You know, Dottie Faye, I'm sorry I let you take the fall

for Bart's death. I planned to pin it on Nate, but you were so conveniently there. No hard feelings?"

"No hard feelings, Priscilla." Dottie Faye moved the brick and reached inside. She gently pulled out the leather bag. "Are you ready to become a millionaire?" She handed it to Priscilla. "Do you want to do the honors?"

In the light of the lantern, Dottie Faye could be seen pulling a pair of handcuffs out of her pants pockets. She reached for Priscilla's wrist.

Mandy screamed, "Watch out, Priscilla! She's lying to you! They're going to get you arrested."

"What'd you do that for?" Nate yelled.

Emma watched the video feed in horror as Dottie Faye and Priscilla began to struggle. Something silver flashed. A knife? Then one of them kicked the lantern into the wall, and it flickered and died.

Dottie Faye was alone in the dark with a killer.

twenty

Emma bolted down the tunnel, fear for her aunt lending wings to her feet. Gruesome images of Dottie Faye being stabbed flitted through her mind like pieces of a bad dream. Only this was all too real.

Behind her, she heard shouts and other footsteps pounding.

A gunshot rang out, the blast echoing through the tunnel like rolling thunder.

Emma ran faster. Had Dottie Faye brought a gun? That had not been discussed.

She rounded the tunnel intersection and skidded to a stop. In the dim glow of her penlight, she saw two figures struggling and rolling on the floor.

"You aren't going to get the best of me this time." Priscilla's face was demented with rage as she bit and clawed and kicked at Dottie Faye. The knife was on the ground and Emma kicked it out of reach of the madwoman. She didn't see Dottie Faye's gun—not that she would have fired it—but she did see something else.

A brick. The one used to hide the treasure.

Priscilla's hands were around Dottie Faye's neck. Dottie Faye gagged and choked, pulling frantically at them.

Almost without thought, Emma bent, scooped up the brick, and whacked Priscilla on the head hard enough to distract her. Dottie Faye quickly detached Priscilla's hands the rest of the way and pushed her off onto the floor. Then Emma and Dottie Faye tackled her and forced her to lie facedown.

They were holding her down and putting the cuffs on when the glow of lights announced the arrival of the others. Nate held Mandy by one arm.

"What took you so long?" Emma said. Priscilla safely secured, she stood and then almost fell as the adrenaline surge faded and the full impact of what had happened hit her. Eric caught her, steadying her with his hands on her shoulders. "Oh, I can't believe I did that," she said, covering her face with her hands. She shuddered. "I've never hit anyone."

Kelly helped Dottie Faye as she straightened from a kneeling position. "It's amazing what you can do when a loved one is at risk," Kelly said.

Dottie Faye held out her arm, displaying a slashed sleeve. "As you can see, she tried to get me." Dottie Faye shook her head sadly. "No honor among thieves. She was going to take the treasure for herself, I'm sure."

"You had a gun," Priscilla said, still lying on the tunnel floor. She rolled over and struggled to a sitting position. "Call the police. I'm pressing charges. Assault with a deadly weapon." She spat on the floor.

Dottie Faye laughed. "Really? We have it all on tape, Miss Priscilla. You're going down for your brother's murder. And by the way, my gun is loaded with blanks. I know better than to fire bullets in a tight enclosure like this."

"I'm glad to hear that," Eric murmured, his eyes wide. Despite her wobbly feelings, Emma smiled. Spending time with Dottie Faye often came with surprises.

"You're in trouble too," Nate said to Mandy. "What were you thinking?"

Mandy ducked her head and sniveled. "I don't know. I'm sorry." Nate dropped her arm. Before he could stop her, she grabbed the bag of "treasure" and took off toward the Tolliver mansion.

"Let her go," Emma said. "That bag is full of fakes."

"What?" Priscilla screeched. "Where is my real treasure?"

Nate smiled. "It's in a safe place. And it's not yours, Priscilla. It belongs to me and the Historical Society."

Kelly pulled out her phone and peered at it with her flashlight. "No signal, of course, since we're underground. Where should I go to call the police?"

"The mansion's closest," Nate said. Reaching down, he helped Priscilla to her feet, treating her gently despite all the evil she had done. "Let's go."

"I'll get the equipment," Eric said. He turned to Emma. "Want to help me? If you feel up to it, of course."

She ignored Kelly and Dottie Faye's smirks. "I'm fine." To the others, she said, "We'll meet you in the kitchen."

Spinelli and his two officers, Soares and Perkins, had arrived by the time Emma and Eric had carried all the equipment up through the basement into the mansion.

"I heard that you got a confession," Spinelli said. "Decided to save the people the cost of a jury trial, Mrs. Sinclair?"

Dottie Faye huffed. "Not me." She pointed at Priscilla, sitting in a chair and still handcuffed. Someone, probably Nate, had duct taped her ankles to the chair. "She killed Bart. And we recorded her confession."

"They're lying. Help me, detective." Priscilla tried to hop the chair across the floor and almost fell over. Eric steadied her.

"Really? Who heard this confession?"

"Oh, about five of us. Six counting our fugitive, Mandy," Emma said.

"Fugitive?" Spinelli frowned.

"It's a long story," Kelly said. "We'll just show you."

"Please excuse me a moment," Emma said. "Restroom." She had to put the bloodstained shirt back where they'd found it. As she ran out of the room, she heard Nate switch on the audio and video files for the policemen. The quality was quite good, Emma realized, despite the challenges of recording underground.

Up in the bedroom, she found the evidence bag holding the shirt. Careful not to touch it again, she opened the bag and dumped the shirt onto the armoire floor. As Emma left the room, she looked at the intarsia quilt with regret. It was highly unlikely they would get to finish it.

"Who fired the gun down there?" Spinelli asked as Emma returned to the kitchen. "That was a gun I heard on the recording, right?"

"You never give up, do you?" Dottie Faye said. "It's mine. It's registered, and I've got a carry permit. And I used blanks." She reached into her pants pocket and pulled out the firearm.

With a nod from Spinelli, Soares took Dottie Faye's gun. Responding to another of his apparently communicative nods, Perkins ripped off the duct tape while reading Priscilla her rights.

"We'll be taking the computer as well," Spinelli said.

"It's an old one," Nate said. "Keep it as long as you want."

"Don't forget the knife Priscilla tried to slash Dottie Faye with," Emma said. "It's still down in the tunnel. And we found a shirt upstairs that we think was worn during the murder. We'll show it to you."

"I'll send the crime team techs over," Spinelli said. "Soares, you wait here."

"Yes, sir." The female officer sat at the kitchen table to wait.

As Perkins helped Priscilla to her feet, she had to get the last word. "Get out. All of you. Get out."

"We'll leave right away, detective," Nate assured Spinelli. "But we've all got personal things we need to get out of here."

"And we need to show the techs the evidence," Emma pointed out.

"You keep an eye on them, Soares," Spinelli said. With a final scowl, he exited.

"I don't think your boss is too happy that we solved the murder ourselves," Kelly said to Soares.

"Don't mind him. He's always like that," Soares said. But the quirk of her lips suggested she agreed.

"Anyone want coffee?" Nate asked. "I know I could use a cup." He went to the counter and filled the coffee carafe with water.

Dottie Faye sagged into a chair, fanning herself. "I suppose I should give Cortland Cabot a call and let him know the news." She found her handbag under the table and pulled out her phone. "Hmm. I have a text." She laughed. "Olivia is innocent. I was wondering when we'd find out."

Nate, standing with his back to them as he spooned coffee into the filter, didn't see Dottie Faye reading the phone. "Of course she is. You never really suspected her, did you?"

Only Emma and Kelly knew what Dottie Faye was talking about. "No, we didn't, Nate," Emma said quickly, to cover her aunt's blunder. "But all leads have to be checked out. We're glad she wasn't involved." Inwardly, Emma sighed. Actually, she would have been glad to finally solve Rose's murder. Now everything rested upon finding Danielle Moore.

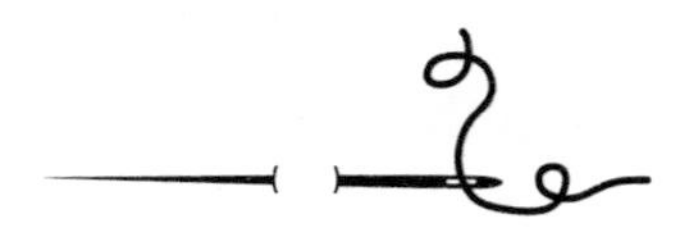

"You look stunning, sweet pea," Dottie Faye said. She looked rather fetching herself in a pale pink shirtdress with matching wide-brimmed hat and pumps, regalia she considered suitable for an award ceremony covered by the press. A tide of voices rose from the store below as friends, customers, and family gathered.

Gazing into the apartment's full-length mirror, Emma twitched the skirt of her coral linen shift into place. "You think?" She picked up a lacy bolero and slipped it on. "I don't know why I'm nervous."

"Because it's not every day you get a national award. Of course, in my eyes you qualify for one at least weekly," Dottie Faye said with a fond smile.

Emma gave a reluctant laugh as Kelly came clattering up the stairs, noisy in the heels she rarely wore. Her swishy teal silk skirt deepened the blue of her eyes. "Ready, Emma? The Preservation Alliance people are here." Her gaze fell on her handbag thrown on the daybed along with Emma and Dottie Faye's. "I should get my phone and have Julie take video with it. I'm so glad she was able to make it home from college for the presentation." The phone rang just as she fished it out, making her drop it onto the bed.

"Let that go to voice mail," Dottie Faye said. "We should go down."

Kelly snatched it up. "It's Alex." She glanced at Emma as though asking what to do.

"Let's take it. He might have news. Can you tell everyone we'll be right there, Dottie Faye?"

"Don't keep your audience waiting too long," Dottie Faye ordered as she swept toward the stairs.

"Alex," Kelly said, putting him on speakerphone as usual. "What's up?"

"Did you find Danielle?" Emma asked.

He sighed heavily. "Sort of."

"Pick up the pace, Alex. Emma and I are late for a very important meeting."

"Well, OK then." The detective sounded slightly offended. "I found out she changed her name to Mary Jones. Talk about a lack of imagination."

"Did you find out where she is?" Emma asked.

"I think I've got her pinned down. I've been following her trail from job to job. Let me check a couple more things, and I'll get back to you."

"Please, do that." Kelly disconnected. "Well, that's promising. Let's go."

"Mary Jones. She couldn't have picked a more common name." Emma followed Kelly down the stairs.

"I suppose that was the point." At the foot of the stairs, Kelly took a deep breath. "We're on."

The store was packed with well-wishers, and Emma realized the estimate of a hundred attendees was close to accurate. At the back of the room, in front of the real potholder quilt, a man and woman from the Preservation Alliance stood with Dottie Faye and Marcia. As Emma made her way through the crowd, she heard someone say, "Congratulations, Emma." She turned to see Eric and Riley beaming at her. He reached out and squeezed her hand while Riley hugged her around the waist.

"I'll talk to you guys later," Emma promised. Somehow their warm support made her feel less nervous. What was there to be afraid of anyway? She was surrounded by friends.

The award ceremony and presentations went off perfectly. Marcia spoke about Emma and Kelly and why she nominated their work. The Preservation Alliance people gave a short history of their organization, and then explained the importance of the potholder quilt to American history and the stellar conservation job Cotton & Grace had done. A representative from the Massachusetts Heritage Society gave a few words of appreciation. The mayor of Mystic Harbor was amazingly brief, and then the award was presented.

Emma was proud of herself for not crying when she and Kelly thanked everyone. The crowd broke into cheers and applause as they held the engraved crystal award up, camera flashes going off all over the room.

Dottie Faye stepped forward. "Thanks for coming, everyone," she said, signaling the end of the formal program.

Everyone milled around and broke into smaller groups while Emma and Kelly shook some hands. The Preservation Alliance and Heritage Society people stayed long enough to meet all the Nimble Thimbles, the mayor, and a few other dignitaries, and then slipped away and headed back to Boston.

"Congratulations." Olivia Stewart pushed through the throng, followed by Nate.

"You do beautiful work," Nate said, examining the potholder quilt. For a change, he had left his plaid flannel shirt at home, and his hair was combed.

He looked like a new person, Emma realized. "It's a shame we won't be able to finish the Tolliver quilt. That is such a stunning piece."

"Oh, but I want you to," he said.

At Emma and Kelly's puzzled looks, Olivia said, "Nate has big news. Go on; tell them." She giggled. "I do too."

Nate glanced around at the crowd and lowered his voice. "The historical society is going to use their half of the treasure to purchase the house and the exhibits once the estate is settled. So, Bart will get his museum after all. I'll make sure they ask you to finish the quilt."

Dottie Faye arrived in time to hear this announcement. "That's just wonderful." Tears sprang to her eyes. "Dear Bart would be so happy."

Everyone was silent for a moment. Then Olivia said, "We'll have a memorial service for him later this summer. Maybe you'd like to help plan it, Dottie Faye?"

Dottie Faye wiped the tears away with a lace-trimmed handkerchief. "I'd be honored."

"What's your news, Olivia?" Kelly asked.

"Bart wrote a codicil that forgave my loan. The lawyer forgot to file it. So, I'm free and clear!"

After a flurry of hugs and handshakes, the Stewarts left with promises to stay in touch.

Emma and Kelly continued to circulate, speaking to everyone and answering questions about their work and inventory. Dottie Faye and Holly, stationed at the counter, rang up sales. Maeve made sure everyone was fed and watered. The event was winding down when Eric approached, his daughter Riley in tow.

"May I see your award, Emma?" Riley asked.

Emma showed it to her, set in pride on a shelf below the wall clock. "See how they engraved our names, the award we received, and the date?"

"Wow. I hope I win an award someday." Riley's eyes were huge.

"You won a blue ribbon at riding camp," Eric said.

"You did? That's amazing, Riley."

Riley ducked her head and twisted one sneaker into the rug. "Yeah. I put my horse through her paces. Walk, trot, and canter. Then we had to stand real still." She nodded her head. "She was a good horse."

"You'll have to show me your blue ribbon," Emma said.

"Maybe when we go on the whale watch."

Riley's mouth dropped open. "A whale watch? Yay!" She clapped her hands.

The pager at Eric's waist went off. "Oops. I've got to go. I'm on call." He gave Emma a rueful glance. "I was going to take you to lunch to celebrate. Rain check?"

"Definitely. See you two later." She watched as they worked their way through the thinning crowd. Maybe she should see what was left on the refreshments table. Now that the excitement was over, she felt quite hungry.

Kelly came up to her. "Look who just showed up." She nodded toward the front door where a familiar tall, bald figure was talking to Tokala and Walter. Antonio Roman, the famous fabric designer. He was dressed appropriately for a gentleman summering at the shore, wearing white linen trousers and shirt accented by expensive-looking boat shoes.

"I wonder what *he's* doing here." Emma shuddered, remembering his smarmy and overly friendly manner when they'd met on a quilting cruise.

"I have no idea," Kelly said.

Antonio Roman raised his head, and with a final word to their friends, he headed toward them, a big smile on his face. "Emma. Kelly. How are you? I was visiting friends on the Cape when I heard about your little event, so I thought I'd offer my congratulations in person." Instead of shaking hands, he held theirs between his two large ones. "It's quite an honor to be recognized by the Preservation Alliance. I'm going to mention it on my website. Perhaps a little blog post highlighting the success of one of my vendors." Like many people with big egos, he made everything about himself.

"Thank you, Antonio," Emma said. Despite her general distaste for the man, she felt a little flutter of excitement. His website got millions of hits, and being featured on it would only help Cotton & Grace.

"Your new line is fabulous," Kelly said. "We're going to place a big order." Kelly knew the value of keeping on Antonio Roman's good side too.

"Good. Good." Antonio craned his neck around, checking out the shop. Then he leaned even closer. "I'd like to take you ladies out to lunch. My way of helping you properly celebrate. I've heard good things about the Hawthorne House."

"The Hawthorne House? Great! I'm starving." Kelly loved eating there, although they rarely did since it was the most expensive place in town.

Emma let Dottie Faye, Maeve, and Holly know where they were going, and they slipped out.

Once settled in the restaurant, cozy with its fine antique furniture and flickering oil lamps on each linen-covered table, Antonio insisted that they order an indulgence, baked stuffed lobster. Unlike boiled lobster, this dish didn't require breaking the crustacean apart and spewing water all over the place.

"All right, if you insist," Kelly said, her eyes twinkling. "I'll also have oyster stew to start."

Antonio ordered the same thing, Emma had a side salad, and everyone had iced tea to drink. The starters came quickly, to Emma's relief. For once, she really *was* hungry.

"I just adore shellfish," Antonio said, spooning up rich broth and succulent oysters. "My poor friend is allergic to them. Quite a drag for someone who lives on the ocean."

"I know someone who's allergic to butter." Kelly shuddered. "Can you imagine?" She was making short work of her bowl of stew.

"Lobster would be pretty bland without it." Antonio took a pull on his iced tea straw. "My only allergy is coffee."

"Really?" Kelly groaned. "I would be doomed. I live on coffee."

"She does," Emma concurred. "And chocolate."

"True." Kelly put her spoon down and foraged in the breadbasket for a hot roll, which she buttered liberally.

"Tell me, ladies," Antonio said. "Are you having any luck with the Rose Peterson case?" When they'd met him on the cruise and explained their quest, he'd expressed great sadness about Rose's death.

Emma put her fork down, suddenly not as hungry. "We're actually down to our last suspect. Danielle Moore." *And if she's not a DNA match, we'll be out of options.*

His eyes sharpened with interest. "Ah. Danielle. I remember her quite well. She had a young child. How is she?"

"We don't know. She changed her name and moved away."

"That sounds suspicious." He sat back in his chair as the waitress served their piping hot lobsters. After they were all set and the waitress was gone, he continued. "So you were able to track her down?"

"Not yet." Kelly dug out a forkful of lobster tail and crabmeat stuffing. "Our detective is on the trail. We'll know soon."

"Great." Antonio wiped his mouth with a cloth napkin. "Let me know if I can be of assistance. I want nothing more than to bring Rose's killer to justice."

The subtle change in his tone caused Emma to look up from her plate. She caught the strange look on Antonio's face before he quickly masked it with his usual smug expression. Something about his behavior didn't seem right—even for one as narcissistic and eccentric as Antonio. *Or am I just imagining things?*

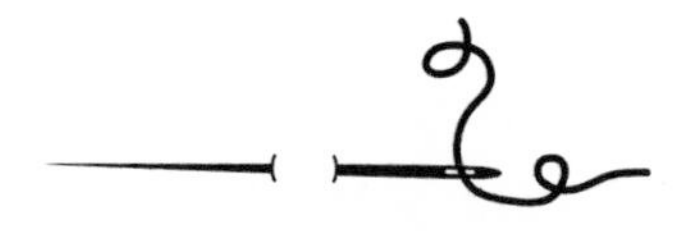

Later that evening, Emma sat on her porch swing enjoying the soft summer dusk. The air was warm and still, the only sound was the swish of a neighbor's lawn sprinkler. Stars twinkled in a velvet sky.

She heard a scrabbling sound in the bushes, and Ichabod ran onto the porch and jumped up on her lap, purring. "Where have you been, little guy? Chasing critters?" Rocking back and forth slowly, she stroked the cat's silky fur and thought about the events of the past few days. This was her first opportunity to relax in quite a while.

And for the first time in a year, she felt comfortable in her own home. The prowler was in jail and no longer a threat. *Maybe Boyer will reopen Rose's case now that he's forced to realize that Kelly and I were right all along. Rose was murdered, and there was a cover-up. Why else would two prominent citizens break the law attempting to stop our investigation?*

With a sigh, Emma shrugged off the bad memories caused by the prowler's harassment and turned her thoughts to more pleasant topics. The award ceremony, for instance. The whole event had been wonderful, a memory she could cherish the rest of her life. And then the day was topped off by a relaxing lunch with a famous textile designer. She'd eaten so much delicious food, she hadn't even thought about cooking dinner. A glass of almost-sweet tea was enough. She reached for the glass on the table beside the swing.

But something about her latest encounter with Antonio Roman kept niggling its way through the glow of the day and back into her thoughts. What was it about that guy that kept her hackles up? Was it something he said? Or was it just something about the way he oozed superiority?

Emma shook her head. She picked up Ichabod, scratching him gently behind the ears. The kitten purred loudly in response.

The latest round in her investigation was ending. But dawn would come quickly, and with it the next chapter in her quest.

"We're going to bring your killer to justice, Rose," she whispered. "Any day now. I just know it."

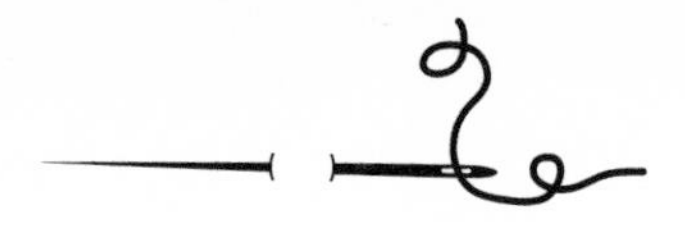

Mystery Sampler Quilt

Create your own mystery sampler quilt with blocks designed by Emma and Kelly and inspired by each book in the series! You'll find a Cotton & Grace block pattern in every Annie's Quilted Mysteries book. At the end of the series, the last pattern will include finishing instructions that will tell you how to stitch the unique blocks together to create a beautiful, one-of-a-kind quilt.

Colonial Garden

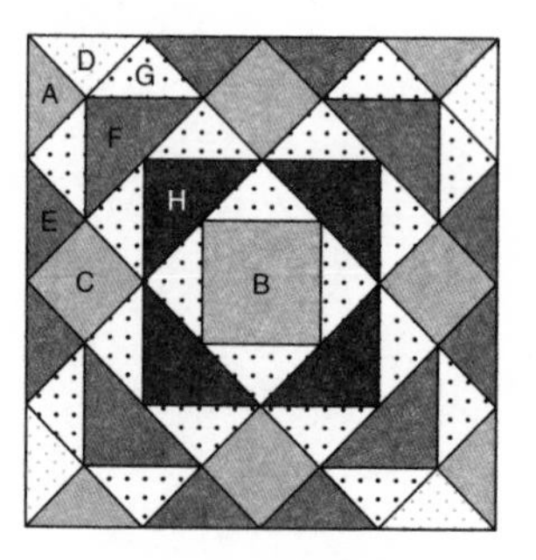

Colonial Garden
12" x 12" Finished Block

Specifications
Finished Block Size: 12" x 12"
Skill Level: Intermediate

Cutting

From Light 1 Fabric:
Cut 1 (4¼") square.
Subcut in half on both diagonals to make 4 A triangles.
Cut 1 (3½") B square.
Cut 4 (2⅝") C squares.

From Light 2 Fabric:
Cut 1 (4¼") square.
Subcut in half on both diagonals to make 4 D triangles.

From Medium 1 Fabric:
Cut 2 (4¼") squares.
Subcut on both diagonals to make 8 E triangles.
Cut 2 (3⅞") squares.
Subcut each square on 1 diagonal to make 4 F triangles.

From Medium 2 Fabric:
Cut 5 (4¼") squares.
Subcut each square on both diagonals to make 20 G triangles.

From Dark Fabric:
Cut 2 (3⅞") squares.
Subcut each square on 1 diagonal to make 4 H triangles.

Assembly

1. Stitch a G triangle to opposite angled sides of an F triangle to make a flying geese unit referring to Figure 1. Repeat to make four G-F units. Set aside.

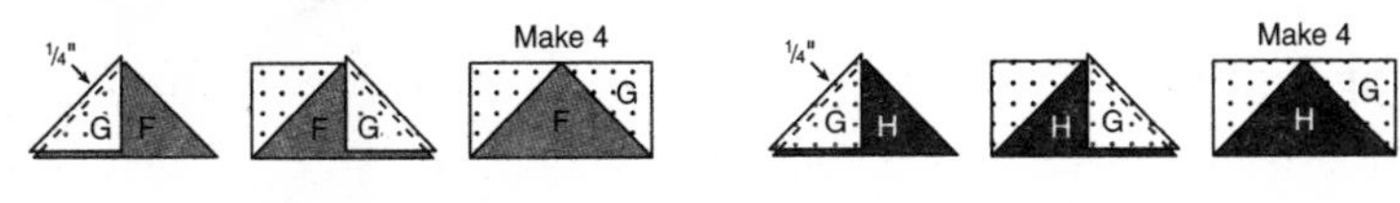

Figure 1 **Figure 2**

2. Repeat step 1 with G and H triangles to make four G-H flying geese units referring to Figure 2. Set aside.

3. Stitch A and D triangles together referring to Figure 3 to make four half-square units. ***Note:*** *Trim seam allowance even with unit side.* Set aside.

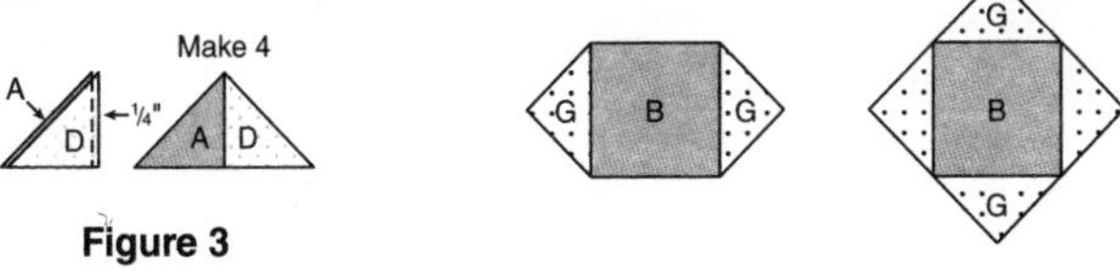

Figure 3

Figure 4

4. Stitch a G triangle to opposite sides of the B square (Figure 4). Stitch a G triangle to remaining sides of B creating block center and referring again to Figure 4.

5. Stitch together two each G-H, G-F and A-D units with the block center referring to Figure 5 to make block center row.

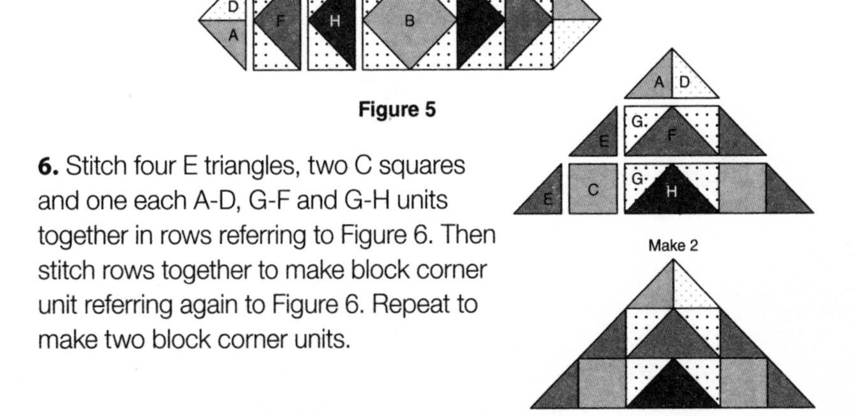

Figure 5

6. Stitch four E triangles, two C squares and one each A-D, G-F and G-H units together in rows referring to Figure 6. Then stitch rows together to make block corner unit referring again to Figure 6. Repeat to make two block corner units.

Figure 6

7. Referring to Figure 7, stitch corner units to block center row to complete Colonial Garden block.

Figure 7

HELPFUL HINTS

• Choose light, medium and dark fabrics for this block. Use scraps from other projects or purchase fat eighths (9" x 22") or fat quarters (18" x 22") to make one sampler block.

• Cut individual pieces from scraps, or cut strips and then individual pieces from strips if using yardage or large pieces of fabric. For example, to cut several 1⅞" squares, cut a 1⅞"-wide strip the width of the fabric. Subcut the strip into 1⅞" squares.

• Use a ¼"-wide seam allowance for all seams and stitch with right sides together.

• For more detailed help with quilting techniques, go to QuiltersWorld.com and choose Quilting Basics under Quilt Essentials, or consult a complete quilting guide. Your local library may have several on hand that you can review before purchasing one.

Annie's Quilted Mysteries™

COMING SOON!

UNRAVELED SECRETS

Emma, Kelly, Dottie Faye, and Maeve team up on two separate leads that they hope will lead them to Danielle Moore, the last suspect on their list of Rose's former students. Will they wrap up their investigation, or will the latest trail end up as so many other loose threads?

Don't miss the next book in this exciting new series from Annie's Quilted Mysteries!